The Evil Genius

Stories

Alan Carmichael

First published 2020
This edition published 2020

© Alan Carmichael   2020

All rights reserved

No part of this publication may be reproduced, stored in a retrieval system, or transmitted in any form or by any means, without the prior permission in writing of the author.

This book and the stories inside are works of fiction. Any resemblance to actual persons, living or dead, is purely coincidental.

ISBN 9-798663-924184

www.thereluctantthief.co.uk

By the same author

The Reluctant Thief
The Gift
The Writers' Group

To Rick and Dee.

For the open road. And much, much more.

Contents

Kathryn's Invitation	1
Winter in the City	15
Crossings	21
A Private Moment	27
A Christmas Ghost Story *or*	
The Evil Genius	29
Eudaimonia	45
Tears	47
Genghis Khan	51
Eudaimonia	79
The Writers' Group	81
Supper at Walter and Jane's	91
The Room	111
Freeway	113
The Escape	117

Author's Note.

These stories were written in the early noughties when I was still learning (or failing to learn, some might say) the craft of writing. Readers may notice the absence of certain features of modern life such as satnav and Wikipedia.

Initially I planned to re-write the stories from scratch. Re-reading them more recently, however, it seemed to me that for all their weaknesses there were one or two strengths as well.

I have decided therefore to leave them unchanged.

Kathryn's Invitation

I had not been particularly keen to attend the awards ceremony, despite the encouragement of my agent, a lady whose considerable charms and a voice many mistook for a certain linchpin of Radio 4 were more usually deployed to soothe the febrile concerns of her romantic novelists.

I had not won a prize. My own publications, dealing as they did with price cycles of competing asset classes in the commodity markets, while well received on Wall Street and at the LSE, were less suited to the champagne and celebrity which, I imagined, might more accurately reflect the tone of the evening.

'Elliott, do come. It will be such fun,' she purred. 'Besides, you need to see how the rest of the publishing industry works.'

'Hmm. It sounds a bit X Factor to me,' I said.

'Elliott, my dear, don't be such a snob.'

To this I made no response. I suspected however that she did have an aim in mind, and that this involved steering me in the direction of those TV academics whose books with their punchy subtitles and the reduction of their disciplines to personalities and bullet-points had transformed the popular science listings - in the process either democratising the academic world or dumbing it down, according to one's view.

'Your money markets. Those hedge funds, those derivatives. It's all mainstream now,' she exclaimed. 'This recession's hit every one of us. God knows. Even I had to let staff go.'

I found myself imagining my next front cover - bloodied titles over graphs of plunging stock markets.

She sent me two tickets - *'But it's fine if you come on your own'* - and a promise that taxis to and from would be arranged. On the back of her card she had written the web address.

The event was to be held in the ballroom of a London hotel, and a graphic showed a dozen circular tables, booked at some expense, it seemed, by leading publishers and agencies, all arranged beneath a raised stage with an oblong bench for judges and hosts. It might have been the seating plan for a society wedding. Black tie was optional. The estimation was, no doubt, that dress codes for recalcitrant authors could never be enforced.

The website listed the award categories and I began to scan the shortlists. Some of the candidates were familiar by reputation, many were not. But halfway down I paused.

Kathryn Spence. *A Mother's Rebirth.*

Underneath, it said, 'One woman's struggle with cancer, a failed marriage, and a drop-out teenage daughter.' The category was Memoir and Autobiography, and I imagined equal measures of misery and triumph-over-adversity, the type of literary mélange which, these days, provided the perfect escape from the rigours of the morning tube from Hendon into the City. There was a photograph, a handsome woman in a white silk blouse with close cropped black hair, one arm around a young woman in a jean jacket, the daughter, now reconciled, one assumed. But I paused for other reasons. The name meant something to me, I had known another Kathryn Spence. For a moment I struggled to visualise this other Kathryn, my Kathryn, and felt, just momentarily, an irritation that it was now so difficult. Brown hair. Yes, she had had light brown hair, I was sure of that. And full, rounded features. Pretty, very pretty. Not angular, almost pinched, as were the features of the woman in the picture.

There was a short biography. She was fifty-five, the same age as me, and she had been to Durham University between

1977 and 1980, again, like me, although she had studied Law not Economics. After that she had moved to London to pursue a career in fashion journalism and had risen to become managing editor of a number of leading women's magazines until illness cut her career short. Now she had written her book. There were commendations from a variety of figures in the public eye, including one from a tabloid owner famous for his expletive-filled tirades against all who crossed him - 'I met Kathy in her days as a cub reporter, and I always knew she had the balls to come through …'

The balls?

Did my Kathryn have balls? The Kathryn of my university days?

Chutzpah. Perhaps that was the word. Perhaps that was the quality that described her and the circle in which she moved. For there was something taking place, that final year at university, the year we all graduated, the year we all began to study and to study hard for the first time since A levels. There was a kind of regrouping going on, a subtle realignment, one based not on academic prowess but on something more difficult to pin down and yet as easy to detect. It was the division of those who relished the ending of this three-year idyll of late mornings, ivory tower reverie and limitless horizons, from those who feared it. One could detect in the former a self-confidence, an assertiveness, in the latter a nervousness about what was to come, a desire to string out the present for as long as possible.

One got clues from their plans for the summer after finals. Some talked of internships with Goldman Sachs, or three months understudy at an opera festival in Tuscany, or interviews with Saatchi's and McCann's in Wardour Street. For these students, the world was theirs, and while they had relished the languor of their undergraduate years, they were now poised to move on, to take leading parts in the world of things, of money, of power and achievement.

Whereas for their peers, those less blessed with such clarity about the future, there were no plans, except teaching and postgraduate work or another year to retake finals.

One could detect a difference in dress and style. For those whose direction was clear and upwards, the cheesecloth and jeans were gone, to be replaced by pressed chinos and jackets. Some bought suits. For the others, the clothes remained indistinguishable from those of their first year protégés, as if by dressing down they might indefinitely postpone their re-introduction to the adult world.

And where did I fit into this?

I remember I had cut my hair - this was the first time I had visited a barber since arriving in Durham - but this was less to do with impressing prospective employers than because a certain spiky-haired Johnny Rotten had said *fuck* on television. I had also, more by luck than design, moved in with two fellow students who most definitely belonged to the chic pioneers poised to storm the kingdom of the grown-ups. And as a sign of the post-student world which they would soon be inhabiting, they had painted every room in the flat a brilliant white, so drawing a distinct line over the squalor of earlier, freshman bed-sits. In that beautiful flat, on a fourth floor, with a balcony and wide windows, they staged parties where the guests drank cocktails, and where smoking a joint had lost its cool.

Would that be when I first met Kathryn? At one of those house parties? I have a memory of these young gods talking and laughing. No, not laughing. Braying. What was discussed? Career trajectories? Golden handshakes? Postings to Manhattan and Hong Kong? No, that is unfair, that is the gloss of an unreliable memory. But I do remember, in that knot of people, and especially in her, a confidence which I might describe as sexual and yet which I now know is something less easy to categorise. It was not only confidence in the act of sex, but also, much more, an assured awareness of what one might call its transactional power, its use, sometimes playful sometimes serious, as a tool one might deploy for barter or to advance one's position or to engage someone's attention. A toss of the hair, a pursing of the lips, the lingering of a stare for a second longer than was necessary. The promise of our lithe and perfect bodies, so taut, so effortlessly active, not yet slowed down by the accumulation of the aches and irregularities which characterise middle age.

She stared at me, and I remember her steady gaze and her smile. What did she say to me, I who had still not emerged from the diffidence of my schooldays? What might I have said to her?

And yet two days later, as I walked in bright October sunlight to the lecture hall, I heard her voice over my shoulder. Loud, direct - 'Elliott, Elliott' - a shout more than a call. I stopped, we chatted. And then I noticed something which stays with me to this day, something so inconsequential which yet somehow characterises her perfection and unattainability. Do I sound eccentric to recall a detail so slight? Or even a bit weird?

She had expertly applied rouge to her cheeks, and I found myself staring at the left side of her face. That she had done so at all was unusual, for most of the girls did not wear much makeup. It was too expensive, too tiresome to apply, and anyway there was no need for artifice in that unblemished world they inhabited. That she had done so with such skill seemed to invest the moment with something else, some mystery, some deeper purpose. Was she going somewhere special, was she meeting someone important? But no, it was me she had buttonholed, just me, and it was the two of us talking.

She had high cheekbones and perfect skin, and the artfulness of her makeup, while noticeable in its artifice, at the same time revealed something else, something essential, the woman inside the girl, a woman who, in this tiny, tiny act of painted illusion, exuded a sensuousness which, in a flash, multiplied the attraction she radiated. We spoke, and I must have held her gaze, just so as to chat, and yet what I really wanted to do was to admire the perfection of that beauty.

'So will you come?' she said eventually.

'Come?'

'My party.' And she handed me a card with an invitation for the weekend following.

I remember that I did indeed go to her party, though I cannot remember who else was there, or what music was playing, or what the guests wore. It was crowded, she was always active, always the centre of attention, making introductions or pouring drinks, absolutely at ease as a hostess. How desperately would I have wished to steer her into a corner and talk, just the two of us, as we had done for a few seconds on that pavement outside the lecture room. We did converse, just the once, though not by ourselves, but instead in a circle of half-a-dozen, each articulate and self-assured in the way that you can be only when you are twenty-one and have a summer internship at Goldman Sachs and the sheer uncertainty of the world is still its most alluring feature. Once she looked at me and smiled and said, 'Elliott, tell me, what do you think?' But I paused, and the chance was lost, and a half-dozen voices crowded out my own.

I left early. I was drunk. The next morning my flatmates found the invitation torn into four on the kitchen table, an act of juvenile pique for which they mocked me endlessly.

*

My agent had a table, the champagne was good, the conversation agreeable, and the speeches from the podium not over-long.

Kathryn Spence won her prize. Elegant in a simple black dress, she accepted her award, said a few words and glided back to her seat. I could see her now, in the shadows away from the stage, a few tables from our own. Could she be the same woman? It seemed to me impossible that she was not, quite unfeasible that there had been two students with the same name. And yet I could not summon up a clear image of the girl I had briefly known. And, worse, the act of seeing her now muddied what memories I had retained, so that the recollection became replaced by a memory of a memory.

The evening wound on, and I knew that, by myself, I should never have attempted to see her up close. But I had reckoned without the enthusiasm of my agent. 'Come on Elliott, move that butt of yours.' She took my hand and pulled me up from my chair. And so it was that we drifted, table by table, ever closer. Along the way I was introduced to the great and the good. I remembered and forgot a dozen names. I grinned - like a clown it seemed as I caught my reflection in a wall mirror. Once, after a flurry of introductions, I referred to myself by my late father's name, for reasons, the next day, I simply could not fathom. And then, suddenly, there were we. My agent was talking. I was staring like a fool.

'Elliott, this is Kathryn Spence. Elliott?'

She looked at me, a brightness in her eyes which seemed one step short of exhaustion.

'Elliott?'

As if she might be counting the minutes, and the glasses of wine, until she could escape.

'Elliott?'

'I'm sorry,' I said. 'Elliott Manson.' And then, 'Congratulations on your prize.'

'Thanks. Thank you.'

My agent was already moving on, and we stood alone, facing each other. I searched for recognition in her eyes. 'I saw your book in Waterstones,' I said. I was lying. I do not know why. 'I saw it. And I did have a quick glance through.'

'But you didn't buy?' She gave a brief grin.

'I'm sorry. I was heading for - well, actually, another part of the shop. My own book was supposed to be buried away somewhere.'

'What's it called?' she said.

And I looked at Kathryn Spence, this Kathryn. I looked at her cheek and the skin radiating away from it down the left side of her face. It was at first sight sallow, and then I knew that it was the intensity of the artificial light in the auditorium, and on closer examination I saw patches of irregular colour, here and there red, elsewhere brownish. And it sagged, her skin sagged over her lower jaw. She wore no makeup, or at least no makeup that I could see. I could not help wondering whether she plucked the hairs on her upper lip. When she said certain words her jaw seemed to lock, momentarily, and the symmetry of her face became just fractionally misaligned. I wondered what the cancer had been. What the treatment had been. There was a large mole on her shoulder above the line of her dress.

I know I must have been telling her a bit about myself, although I cannot remember exactly what, but she did interject. 'So you were at Durham? When? Perhaps we knew each other.'

I wondered what to say. And while I wondered I prevaricated. 'When were you there?'

She picked up a handful of nuts from a bowl on the table, hesitated, then put them back down again. 'You first.'

Later, much later, when I got home, I stood in front of the bathroom mirror, and I stared at my face. My own skin. Like hers, blotchy. Sallow here, dyspeptically red there. I had shaved unevenly, and there were clumps of grey stubble around my chin. Hairs coming out of my nose. Pores enlarged with the alcohol I had consumed during the evening.

I stumbled out of the room and spent ten minutes searching for old passports. Finally, in a bottom drawer, I found what I was looking for. Myself, face front, the picture taken in 1980. The eyes, without glasses, the skin smooth and tight, the hair black and full, a New Romantic cut.

'You first,' she said once more.

And I funked it. 'I only stayed one year. I dropped out in 1978.'

'That's unfortunate,' she said. 'We might have known each other. We might have met, you know, at parties and things.'

A young woman had joined her and was standing off her shoulder, her eyes alternately holding mine and then glancing down at the profile of the woman I faced. 'Mum,' she said softly. 'You look tired,' and she placed an arm around her mother's shoulders.

Kathryn Spence turned and smiled. At last she appeared to relax. 'Not at all, my dear, not at all.' She reached up and placed a hand over her daughter's. 'Elizabeth, I want you to meet Ev … Ed …'

'Elliott. Elliott Manson.'

'I'm sorry.'

'Don't be. I'm the same. So many names this evening …'

'Do you have children, Elliott?'

For a moment I considered lying once more. Perhaps, because I had already gone this far with my evasion, it was as well to continue. But I didn't. 'Yes, two,' I said. I looked across then at her daughter, and for a moment I studied her makeup, my gaze hurried, as if it might be construed by the elder of the two women as the lechery of an older man. It may have been that in part, yes I admit, but it was also something more, for I was looking, in that eye shadow, in the rouge, for the woman in the child, and then, as my eyes returned to her mother, for the child in the woman. Kathryn Spence did not seem unduly bothered by my wondering eye, indeed she may have felt a moment's pride at this beauty at her side and her role in its creation.

'It's amazing, isn't it?' she said.

'What is?'

'To see them like this …' And she placed her other hand around her daughter's waist.

'Oh, Mum. Stop it.'

'Elliott, what do you think?'

I looked at the two of them and I knew that, yes, it was truly amazing.

'Elliott? Tell me, what do you think?

But I never replied. At that moment my agent grabbed me by the arm and propelled me away.

*

A few weeks later my brother invited me to a dinner party at his home. Freddie and his wife Sarah were both excellent cooks, and they knew how to balance a guest list between the familiar - there would be friends we had known since our school days - and the new. On this particular evening, one of the unfamiliar faces was a teaching assistant at the large secondary school of which he was headmaster. She was vivacious, over-qualified - her PhD more than adequate for the sixth form physics she taught - and Polish. I guessed she might break a few hearts amongst the adolescent boys in her charge.

Whether it was my brother's intention that she should also steal mine was less clear. My wife had left me ten years before, taking the two girls with her, and even after this time he could never quite bring himself to accept the fact of my singleness.

'Get out there,' he said to me periodically. 'There's no age limit to dating these days.' I knew he was right.

'What about that bank where you work?' Sarah would add, 'You must be a catch. We're always hearing about you guys making whoopee in the City.'

But on this particular evening it was work not romance which filled the conversation between myself and Agnieska.

'So what exactly is it that you do?' she said. 'How do you make all that money out of nothing?'

And I explained, as I always did, in some detail, although in this case her interest and obvious intelligence made the task considerably easier. I explained that twenty years before, as a researcher supporting one of the large trading floors, I had uncovered an extraordinary and until then unnoticed link between bull and bear cycles in different classes of commodities. I explained how I had verified this link by exhaustive research, and then encoded the rules governing these cycles into a suite of software which had made my company, and others that I subsequently joined, immensely wealthy, and myself at least moderately so. And that these rules were known, the world over, as the *Kastner-Manson Wave*, the *Kastner* referring to my one-time boss, a banker of super-sized ego and remarkable trading skills who got vaporised, along with all twenty members of his team, when at 8:46 AM on a bright morning the first plane crashed into the North Tower.

Perhaps it was the long silence that followed which led to the change of subject. She began to speak about her doctorate and the dissertation she had published.

The quantum mechanics lost me early on, but she soon leavened the conversation with her own speculations about parallel universes. 'I'm quite serious,' she said. 'There really could be a parallel *you* somewhere out there. The physics supports it. Just think. Think of all the things in your life you didn't do. Perhaps somewhere, you *did*.'

But her efforts to persuade me of this were, to my ears at least, less convincing, if only because of the unproveability of the assertion. It seemed like saying there were green men on Pluto. Perhaps there were, but if we could never verify the statement, we were therefore best advised to ignore it.

But as the evening wore on and I thought about it more, it seemed to me there was another, more powerful reason for thinking that her ideas had to be wrong. And I wondered whether such a view came about as a function of age. For it seemed to me, as I looked back on the years, in that living room, sitting across from Freddie and Sarah, that there was an inevitability about our being in this place and in this moment, an inevitability prescribed by the weight of the forces of our personalities which became apparent only as they - and we - settled into our later decades. I thought of myself as a teenager, and how things appeared so marginal, so contingent, so alive with a promise that lay just at the very periphery of my fingertips' grasp. And if some opportunities had been dangled in front of me and later withdrawn, well then others had been seized.

And that was the way it had gone because that was the only way it could have gone.

And I recalled the early years, before the cancer in my marriage became irreversible, and the passion and the tantrums and the parties and the occasional ecstasies. And the two small miracles when Jessica and Maddy arrived. And the first time I saw - yes, even that was a small marvel - that a six figure bonus had been deposited into my bank account. And the first time I saw someone reading my book - with my name on the cover - on the tube going into work.

Jessica and Maddy. Why did we use the diminutive for one and not the other? 'Fred was telling me you have children.' Agnieska was talking again.

I saw Sarah glance across at us. For a moment she held my eye.

'Yes,' I said turning back. 'Two girls.'

Agnieska's eyes widened - a teacher's enthusiasm. 'How old are they?'

'Well, they're ... they're not much younger than you. They are at university.'

Conversation at the other end of the table had subsided.

'Do you have any pictures?' - her Polish accent somehow defusing any embarrassment at the silence - 'I would love to see.'

But here I myself paused for a few seconds, unable to frame a response.

'Right. Coffee. Anyone?' Freddie was standing up.

I had paused because the only pictures I kept in my wallet were of the two of them as young girls, and the truth was that I had nothing more recent than that, because the truth was that I had not seen them, not once, since the day their mother walked out, one child under each arm. And the truth was that they refused to speak to me, to answer my letters or my emails or my phone calls. Because in the catastrophe of our divorce there had to be an angel and a devil, and if the children needed some shred of sanity to hold on to and if some artifice kept alive for them the image of their mother as angel, then I would happily play the devil.

So I paid anonymously for their tuition fees, and the trusts were quietly maintained for the day they turned twenty-one. And sometimes I stayed up late, till three, four in the morning, scanning the webpages of Jessica's drama school or Maddy's law college, searching for clues, for cast lists or productions or public debates, anything which might contain in the fine print some detail of their lives. Because they would contact me one day, of that I was sure. One fine day, perhaps when they were adults and had careers and lovers, or when they had children of their own, when they realised that any final verdict on the decisions people made - even those of their parents - was never quite as unequivocal as the graph of a market's fall.

'They're funny, those boys.' Agnieska had not stopped talking. She was describing her students. 'So funny, all of them,' she said. 'But I love it. I love it at your brother's school.'

Freddie was circulating with a napkin in one hand and, in the other, a bottle of clear Italian liqueur which he poured into tiny iced glasses. I sat, quite still, with my open wallet in my hands, and when Agnieska placed a hand over her glass - she had hardly touched her wine all evening - I saw him lean down and whisper into her ear. She glanced up at me once.

'Agnieska, I hope my husband is not working you too hard,' Sarah called out across the table as Freddie moved on. 'All those teenagers. All that testosterone.'

I folded my wallet and returned it to my jacket pocket.

'Not at all.' Agnieska laughed. 'Not at all.'

Her expression tightened slightly as she turned back to me. 'I mean it,' she said softly. 'I love it there. I really do.' And then she added, 'It's a good life.'

For some reason the phrase startled me. For I had been thinking, as I had done so frequently in the days and weeks since, about my meeting with Kathryn Spence, and why it was that I lied, why it was that I had been so evasive. And I had been thinking also about the questions Kathryn Spence had put to me right at the end as she stood with her arms around her daughter. *It's amazing*, she had said, inviting me to agree. And it came to me, then, the reason I had not responded.

'Don't you think?' Agnieska pressed.

I knew why I had not answered, why I could not find it in myself to answer.

'Elliott?'

But I knew also that one day - one fine day - all that would change.

Winter in the City

They kicked off with tequila slammers straight after work, they moved on to champagne at seven. At nine someone bought a quart of brandy, and they switched to pints of beer as the place began to clear, although Pete had absolutely no recollection of this the following day.

A long, curving bar, brass and chrome, floor to ceiling mirrors and a kaleidoscopic array of bottles, of wines, liqueurs and spirits, labels with gaudy promises of Rio, Havana, Warsaw. They had rushed down at five thirty, they stood eager and huddled, cocktails in hand, though others on early shift had been quaffing lagers for two hours already. Braying crowds, ties loosened, sleeves rolled, wine stains unnoticed on the Armani and Prada. Waiters strutted amongst them, blond giants in aprons and waistcoats, androgynous and beautiful. They looked out from the thirtieth floor at a sky of exquisite and darkening blue, its depths already pierced by the first stars. A plastic tree with lights and baubles stood tucked away in the corner, its ancient promise of the transcendent indiscernible within the sparkle.

Senior managers arrived early evening, corporate credit cards flashing in the beam of the ceiling spotlights, and a roar erupted as corks popped and a stream of *Veuve Clicquot* flowed out and over a stacked row of glasses. Four traders began dancing on the tables, and the head of HR belted out Madonna and Kylie. Someone flashed a wad of fifties, and the bar staff quietly advised other customers to finish their drinks and leave.

The American partners headed for the door with a look of faint disgust. Their French colleagues followed minutes later. *Cochons*, one was heard to mutter, and the head of operations dropped to all fours and scurried up and down the floor, snorting, belching and farting, a dozen colleagues yelping at his side. Inhibitions were tested and forgotten, talk became jagged, belligerent, there were tears in the loo and punch-ups outside. The passage of time seemed to fracture and bend.

Pete joined his friend Jake who sat drinking shorts with a bunch of screaming techies. Fast, fluent, they talked XBoxes and bluetooth, linux and Ipods. The future of mobile telephony.

'We need another bottle,' someone cried.

The hot issue was low-altitude satellites falling out the sky. A waitress sashayed into their orbit.

'The Yanks let 'em burn out over the Pacific.'

She swivelled her hips as Jake reached for an ashtray on the next table. The lads hooted.

'Who's good for credit? I'm maxed out.'

At ten, the room began to empty, dishevelled men and women citing baby-sitters and last trains out to the suburbs. Stragglers stared out over the wreckage of the bar, a visceral craving for alcohol still scratching away inside them. They lurched out into the night only as waiters began to stack chairs.

'Jeez, it's fucking freezing.'

Pete wrapped his arms around his shoulders against the wind. Someone flagged down taxis.

'I know a place in Soho.'

Night enfolded him. Recollection came later in fragments. Two men in suits, supine, unconscious on the pavement. The taxi braking sharply, a gaggle of women shrieking, stumbling across the road in their stockinged feet, strappy heels draped over their shoulders.

They danced in a crowded basement, they drank litres of water and took pills. They hassled girls in black leather and make-up and got thrown out by bald men in suits. Pete and Jake sat alone in an after-hours Chinese and bribed the waiter to serve them booze. They drank wine out of a tea pot, they stared at their food and ate nothing, and then Jake shook Pete by the shoulder.

'Hey, mate, behind you. Look out there. Magic.'

Pete held his head in his hands. For a second he wanted to throw up.

'Hey, man, it's fucking snowing.'

Pete turned. Outside, snowflakes drifted down as if caught in suspension. They piled up on the window ledges. Jake was already rushing for the exit.

'I'm out of here.'

Pete fished out his wallet as three waiters slithered over. He watched Jake through the open door, staring up at the sky, arms raised, rotating on his heels. His shoulders shimmered with a layer of white powder.

'Hey, God, you fuck.' He screamed at the sky. 'So what happened to global warming?'

He burst out laughing, and Pete laughed as well, until he felt sick again. Jake stared upwards, oblivious, now twirling on the balls of his feet.

They walked.

A bridge over the Thames. They sat, legs outstretched, backs against the rail as snow fell over them. They discussed the meaning of life and the size of the tits on the new secretaries. Men of Eastern appearance in battered Volvos stopped and offered to take them home for forty pounds, but Pete and Jake had spent the last of their cash, and the writ of their plastic did not extend to the *demimonde* of fake work permits and asylum claims.

Later.

Sludge on the pavements of Vauxhall and Stockwell. They zigzagged and fell, Jake stopped to throw up. They breathed steam and warmth into their fingers, they cursed that they had left their coats behind. The cold and the churning snow stung their eyes and burnt their cheeks. A blizzard began around them, cars slowed and skidded. Two figures loped out of the gloom, tall, six-six, basketball players in silent duet around an imaginary ball, black silhouettes, white eyes, white trainers, black hoods. Gliding either side and disappearing into the distance.

They reached the Common. They moved away from the streetlights onto the grass, and Jake stooped to pack snow between his hands. He threw a snowball at Pete and ran off. He shouted. 'Hey, there's a pond here somewhere. Let's go ice skating.'

Pete breathed heavily. 'Wait. Wait.' He sank to his knees. He could not go on. It was so dark. For a moment he blacked out where he knelt. He awoke and staggered forward.

'Jake.'

There was ice under his feet. Instantly he stopped.

'Jake.'

He tiptoed and paused. Somewhere, ahead of him, fainter. 'Hey, over here.'

Pete skidded forward two more steps and stumbled. He felt ice break beneath him. His left foot fell six inches and water immediately soaked through his sock. With one foot he waded, feeling slime under his shoe, and his balance again deserted him. He lurched and crashed onto his back, he felt sheets of ice splintering and cracking apart and then freezing slush swirl over his body. He braced himself with his elbows. He lay half submerged. A liquid chill flowed over his torso, his arms, his ankles. He rested, stunned.

I'm going to die tonight ...

He tried to raise himself but could not. A numbness throbbed somewhere in his legs and began to creep upwards to his torso.

I'm going to die tonight unless I get up from here ...

And then his eyes adjusted to the night and in the grey and silver he saw Jake six feet away, face down, his body propped up on elbows and knees, shards of ice scattered about him. He was weeping.

'That bitch.'

Jake shivered violently and thrashed about in the water for a few moments.

'That fucking bitch, why did she do it?' And once more, a whisper this time. 'Why did she do that?'

Pete felt the numbness spreading, and with it came a ghostly calmness, a sense of letting go, an intuition that somehow nothing quite mattered any more.

Jake wept beside him.

I will die. Tonight I will die.

Time stopped. Change ceased. Desire, pain, pleasure, all seemed somehow removed and absent. He rested his neck and stared up. The storm had ended, the sky was miraculously clear. He began to count the stars. One, two, three ... A marvellous and incomprehensible infinity ... Twenty, twenty one, twenty two ...

A star was moving.

Impossible. No. Yes.

It was moving.

He stared. Yes, it was moving. He marked its position in his field of vision against a cluster of other stars and watched. And waited. Slowly, steadily, it passed across the sky. And then he noticed a steady growth and decay in its luminescence, as if it were rotating or reflecting in some programmed cycle, and he knew suddenly it was not part of God's heaven at all.

A satellite ...

He began to laugh. The paralysis had extended to his right arm, his back, his ankles. He raised his left hand to the sky, and stretched and bent his fingers, as if to measure and contain the advancing light that he saw above him. And then – he gasped - a silent explosion. He saw the point of light expand and burst into five, a momentary pentagram of fire, and then each point burn and splutter and begin to fall to earth. He shifted his hand, he picked out the path of one of its threads, and bent his thumb and forefinger into a kind of claw, as if to capture it as it fell. And the pinprick of light flared and began to fade, and as it faded he brought his two fingers closer and closer together, and as it died between them his fingers touched, and for a second he imagined he held its heat and its beauty there, just there, in the folds of his skin.

Pete breathes out.

The sky turns, the night has ended. He sees slivers of blue against the eastern sky. He senses a warmth coming back to him, and almost immediately afterwards a coldness, a freezing wetness and a sting which takes the breath away. But at the same time it is an ecstasy, it is bliss just to feel something, to feel again, and he knows that if he may die one day, it will not be tonight, not here, not in this pond, not by this grassland. He stirs. He speaks.

'Jake.'

He raises himself up amongst the crackling ice and looks around. Jake crouches. He is silent.

'Jake, here, take my hand.'

Pete gets up, staggers, and shuffles over to his friend. 'Take my hand.' He crouches and places an arm around his friend's shoulder.

'It's OK,' he says softly. 'Grab my hand. We're going.' They hold on to each other tightly. 'I'm going to take you home.'

Crossings

'I think I'll go to bed now,' she said. It was seven o'clock.

'You sure?' he said. 'I can read a little while longer.'

He stood and stretched, and then caught himself in the mirror above the mantelpiece. He stooped slightly and shook his head from side to side. The patch just by his crown, thin, wispy, was not quite visible at this distance. It seemed to him as he looked that it was not really visible at all. Only if one paid close attention. He passed a finger through it, and caught a couple of loose hairs which he twirled round his nail and released, and then, caught by a shiver of remorse at his narcissism, glanced down at the old woman on the settee. But she was gazing into space.

'Are you quite sure?' he said.

'Yes. I'm tired now.' She breathed out slowly. 'But you stay up. Enjoy yourself.'

She still did not move.

'Do you need a hand?'

'No.' She reached for the stick which lay against the arm rest, 'No. I have to do this ...' she grunted and heaved, ' ... myself.'

He watched her roll back and forth a few times and then lurch forward into a crouch. He caught her shoulder as she began to topple back. She gripped her stick with her right hand, steadied herself against the coffee table with her left, and began to straighten.

'I can manage,' she whispered. She stood for a moment and then shuffled forward towards the kitchen. He heard steps padding across the lino, a tap running, a glass being filled. A toilet being flushed. The bathroom which they had recently fitted on the ground floor. He found himself wondering whether she would ever see the upstairs rooms again.

He waited a while and then sat down and switched on the television.

She was asleep when he decided to go to the pub.

The light was on by her bed, a hand still gripped a pencil, although the writing pad she had been filling out had slipped to the floor. Her mouth was open, and she snored softly.

He picked up the pad and glanced over it. There was a greeting at the top of the page, a spindly *My Dearest Sister*, and after that the handwriting trailed off into nothing. He tried to read a few words. He made a mental note to buy stamps the next day.

He switched off the lamp and tiptoed out the room.

Outside, the moon was full.

He looked along the street. Every light, in every house, in every living room, was off. Boxy saloons were parked, one after the other, in parallel lines on successive forecourts. In the crushing silence, as he opened the door and started up the engine, he felt eerily guilty.

He sat, one of three customers, in what a sign at the entrance referred to as the lounge bar. He read the paper. A television played in a corner, some soap instead of the football. The barmaid watched from a stool. He did not quite finish his second pint.

He drove along the seafront for a while. A police car followed him for two minutes and then turned off. The glisten of the moonlight on the water for once did nothing for him.

Crossings

After a while he turned back and began to thread his way towards his grandmother's house.

There was a grid of side roads, *Give Way* signs at each intersection. He stopped, looked, accelerated forward fifty yards. Stopped again. Looked. Accelerated. There were no other cars.

He drove towards the house and slowed. *There will be a day*, he thought, *when I will never, ever, have to turn into this drive again*. He imagined another family living there. The thought excited and then repelled him. He swore, and carried on past, over further crossroads to the end of the road where he pulled over. He looked at his watch. It was nine forty-five. He wondered whether Annie might have called, reached into his pocket, and then swore again. His mobile was in his overnight bag.

He swung round and headed for home.

Fuck. He put his foot on the accelerator. *Fuck, fuck, fuck*. He considered, and straight away discarded, the possibility that there were speed cameras on this road. This far out from the centre of town. Surely not. *Fuck, fuck, fuck*. He was doing fifty miles per hour.

'Jesus.' He jerked his foot onto the brake and pressed. The sound of the tyres quite shocking in the silence. The car began to veer to the right, the first crossroads just yards away. 'Jesus.' He was slowing, but skidding, skidding. 'Whoooaaaaa.' The back of the car came swivelling round. He came to a stop.

He breathed out. A dog began to bark. His bonnet protruded two yards out into the crossing. The engine had stalled. He looked left, right, left again. 'Jesus.' And then he sighed. Not a single car. Not one. He began to laugh. A light came on in a house on the corner. He looked up. A curtain fluttered. *Fuck you*, he thought. He switched on the engine and began to edge forward.

He pushed on to the next junction, still laughing. He stopped, looked around and moved forward again. Once more he went past the house and continued to the end of the road where it met the seafront. Once more he u-turned. He stopped and put the gear into neutral.

He looked ahead of him, the road continuing straight, into the shadows beyond the gleam of the streetlights. He began to count the junctions in his head. Three, four up to the house. After that, two more? He closed his eyes, and began to breathe deeply, rhythmically. Then, eyes open, he smiled. He gripped the steering wheel.

You're young. You're not dead yet.

He thought of his grandmother lying on her bed, the webbed structure of her memory loosening, the shards of identity unanchored, adrift. The image came to him of the two wooden clocks on her living room wall. Their porcelain faces. The hands of carved steel. The twin ticking just out of phase. He thought of her neighbours, upstairs in their bedrooms, cocooned, at rest, in hibernation from the night. A rack of Marks & Spencer nightgowns, a pair of slippers. A tumbler of water, a bedside thriller. Her neighbours' neighbours. And theirs.

He was in first, flying, the engine screaming. Rows of houses. Flying. Into second. Row upon row upon row. Forty. Forty-five. He skipped third. Into fourth. It was there, ahead. The first one. The first junction. Fifty yards, thirty, twenty, ten ... flying ... flying ... row upon row ... upon row upon ...

The houses quite suddenly stretched away to nothing. Both right and left. Just road, infinite road to right and left, and ...

Across. He was across. *Fuck.* He pressed down. Fifty, fifty-five. Into fifth. The second junction. Here. Now. *Aigh.* Here. Now. And ...

Over. We're there. Next one. *Slow. Slow down.* Four more. Just four. *No. No. Go for it. Go. Go.* Aigh. *Go ...*

Another one down. *More.* The next one. Just feet away. Needle flickering, sixty-five. *Aagh. Aagh.* Nearly there. Breathe. Breathe in. Out. In. Out. In...

Across. Eyes to the left and the right. Houses again. Abruptly.

Across.

Across.

And then ahead of him, at the edge of the limit of his vision, faint. a beam, raking up and down the road, its pool of light a full hundred yards in front. Dull. Insistent. Brightening. *Slow, slow ... No. Go, go ...*

One left. One to go. The light ahead. *Hey. Hey. Slow down.* Sixty, fifty. A headlamp, flickering somewhere from left of field, there at the next junction. *Shit. Why now?* Decelerating. Fast. *Damn, damn, damn ...* Forty. And then a skid, his heart freezing, a shearing movement, across the road, *Foot off, take it off, foot off, foot off, foot off ...* Traction. Tyres gripping. *Now ...* Slowing ... *press, press ...* Slowing. ... *down.* The other car. Headlights on beam. There they were. Almost in front of him. *Harder.* He saw the driver. Face turning towards him. Passengers. Eyes wide. Mouths open. Their car swinging round left to right across the line of sight in front of him.

Swinging. Swinging. Swinging ...

*

She lay on her back, eyes open, staring up at the ceiling. A side light was on. After a while she twisted slowly, grunted, and looked over to her side. She reached out a hand, picked up the glass of water, and raised it her lips. She sipped, swallowed, and relaxed back onto her pillow.

He watched her from the shadow by the door.

'Did you have a nice drink?' she said.

He moved forward into the light and stood by her table.

'It was quiet.'

'Did you meet any girls?'

'No.' He smiled down at her. 'Not this time.'

She raised her head, took another sip, and then, her hand trembling, spilled a few drops over the bedspread.

'Here. Let me.' He eased the glass from her grip.

'I heard some shouting,' she said.

'Just some driver.'

Her head craned forward, and she looked directly at him. She waited.

'Someone was driving too fast,' he said. She did not look away. 'You know how people are.'

'I hope no one was hurt.'

'No. No one was hurt.'

She continued to observe him. 'One more sip.' She reached out her fingers.

He handed her the glass. She looked at it for a moment, sighed and leaned back. He took it from her.

'You don't have to come,' she said. 'You really don't. You know that.'

'I want to. I do. Of course I do.'

Her eyes closed. 'Good. That's all right then.'

He waited and then he said, 'I'm going to bed now.' But she did not reply. He looked down at her, and then leaned forward, kissed her on the forehead and switched off the lamp at the side of her bed.

A Private Moment

He went through the door, walked a dozen paces, and sat down in front of the glazed keys where he paused for a few seconds to think. His gaze moved across the black wooden surface of the raised lid and he noticed a layer of dust covering a small section. It seemed odd that they should have missed this, and he raised his right forefinger to trace a line through it.

Odd.

Perhaps an omen. He tried to repress the thought but was unable to do so.

His finger remained, taut, poised on the black surface and he smiled at his superstition.

At that moment he was aware of a movement to his right side.

He looked, tried to see, but, apart from a shadowy form in the near distance, could make out nothing. Instead the space seemed to extend to a distance at once incalculable and intimate. Had this been the intention of a long dead architect?

If he could not see, however, he could, as his senses strained, hear. A cough, a sigh, a body shifting. A tension. A hint of embarrassment at the lengthening silence.

He smiled again, then looked once more at his fingers which he stretched, studied and twisted. He wore no rings. There was a callus on the third finger of his left hand and he rubbed it gently with his right thumb. The movement was circular, the touch light and barely felt. He stretched his hands one more time and then laid them on the keyboard.

Two thousand people watched him as he did these things. He began to play.

A Christmas Ghost Story   *or*

The Evil Genius

'So I could be ****ing with your mind?'
'What did you say?'

Mike Wallis turned from the whiteboard and looked across at the class. There was silence. Twenty-eight boys stared at him and waited.

'Just what did you say?' the teacher repeated, and this time his gaze was directed at Thomas Ephis who sat second from the back in the third row.

'I could be messing with your mind, sir?' the boy said. 'If, that is, I was the evil genius.'

There was a squeaking of chairs, a few sniggers, and then Mike Wallis smiled himself and the tension broke.

'Yes, Thomas, I suppose you could. *If* you were the evil genius.'

In twenty years in the classroom Mike Wallis had learned that there were times when you had to assert your authority, forcefully, sometimes even with the slightest risk of being arbitrary and mean. But there were also times when it was best to bend with the prevailing mood, to accept the occasional challenge to your status. To appear human. And with Christmas a week away and term wrapping up the next day, this was one of those occasions.

In fact he had done well to get this far, forty minutes into the lesson, without losing the boys' interest and with no serious breakdown in discipline. He took this as being due in part to his skill as a teacher, and also to his practice of digressing from the standard curriculum for the final two or three classes.

The lower sixth had done as much maths as was required for the term, and it was his custom, with that milestone passed, to shake things up with a quick foray into one or two of the byways of philosophy and mathematics which, he hoped, might just fire up the interest of the brightest as they considered university.

The theme for the lesson had been reality itself - the reality of the universe around us. And whether we could take that reality for granted.

This was aiming a touch high for some - 'Hey. It's there. Get over it,' one boy whispered early on. Yet Mike Wallis' tone was breezy, and, as he had expected, indeed hoped, not beyond the odd bit of light mockery.

He had started with The Copenhagen Doctrine of quantum physicists Bohr and Heisenberg, who argued that quantum reality, the stuff of the universe, was somehow predicated on the observations of a quantum observer. He moved from there to the paradox of Schrödinger's hypothetical cat, simultaneously alive and dead.

He proceeded at pace to the Idealism of Bishop Berkeley and his precept "to be is to be perceived", and rounded off with René Descartes, the first among Western thinkers to understand that the Thing was different from the Perception of the Thing.

'Imagine, therefore, some malignant and all-powerful being.' His tiring pupils, he could see, were beginning to cast surreptitious glances at concealed mobile phones. He raised his voice a fraction. 'Some evil genius who *steps between Thing and Thought*, who deliberately falsifies every piece of sensory information your mind receives …'

The murmuring in class was becoming louder in expectation of the bell.

'… who feeds you a stream of illusion about an external world …a world that is just not there …'

The Evil Genius

He clapped his hands.

'Boys, boys. Just a couple more secs. Tell me, one last question, what phrase is Descartes famous for? Anyone? In English? Cogito, ergo …'

Quick as a flash, 'I drink, therefore I am.'

More quietly, 'I wank, therefore I am.'

Mike Wallis shook his head, waved his hand lazily towards the door, and turned to erase the whiteboard. There was a rush of desks slamming, of teenagers grabbing bags, shouting, running for the door.

'Happy Christmas,' he yelled without turning, 'Happy, happy, happy …'

He sighed. A silent classroom. Another term. Another year. How many more would there be? He began to collect his papers. And then paused.

There was one boy still in the room. He stood waiting at Mike Wallis's table. It was Thomas Ephis.

'Happy Christmas, sir.' He extended his right hand. In it he held a white envelope. For a moment Mike Wallis was unsure how to react.

'Well I …'

The boy laid the envelope on the table. 'Happy Christmas,' he said again. 'I've got you a card.' He smiled a seductively bright smile - it lasted a fraction of a second - and then turned and walked to the door.

Mike Wallis scratched his head and watched him. As the boy walked out and let the door swing shut, he recovered his poise. 'Well, thank you. Thomas, that's generous, that's very …'

His voice echoed. The room was empty.

*

Arthur Goldstone, another of the old-timers and, in his spare time, general secretary of the Society for the Protection of the

Apostrophe, was complaining as he often did about the erosion of good manners in the pupils.

Mike liked Arthur, even if the younger teachers took pains to avoid him. The two had started out together a generation before, and that shared history counted for something, But today he had to demur.

'Arthur, I actually got a Christmas card from one. That shows some thought.'

'One? Out of how many?'

'Er, twenty-eight.'

'Point proved. Here, let me see.'

Mike had not in fact looked at the card himself. He ripped open the envelope. On the front of the card was a detail from a Breughel painting. Hunters traipsing across a Flemish snowscape. Mike had always found Breughel's images disturbing. The painter's characters seemed to him on the very edge of the grotesque.

Inside was a greeting, 'Merry Christmas', and then - curiously, one signature under the other - the boy's name written twice.

'Who's it from?'

'Thomas Ephis. Know him?'

'Hmm. No. Ephis, what is that? Greek?'

Mike handed across the card. His colleague stared down his bifocals.

'Good Lord, does he need practice with his own name? He's signed it more than once. What's that all about?'

Mike took back the card, but didn't reply. His phone was vibrating. Arthur, the only person Mike knew who resisted owning a mobile, looked away in distaste.

Mike stood up and put the phone to his ear. 'Maureen,' he said quietly. 'How're things?'

He walked over to the far side of the room and looked out the window. Sky clear blue, diamond sharp. Black outlines of leafless trees across the football field, hyper-real in their clarity.

The Evil Genius

'Darling?' He could hear his wife moving about. He was surprised, and glad, that she was out of bed. He knew that sometimes she slept all day. Her doctor had prescribed pills. She had been devastated by the recent deaths, one after the other, of her parents.

'I'll be back soon,' he told her. 'Not much on this afternoon.' He waited. She talked. 'OK, dear,' he interjected repeatedly. 'I'll be leaving early, don't worry. Love you.' He wondered whether he might actually be able to drive home in the daylight.

And then he remembered his car. The car park had been full when he arrived, and street parking allowed a maximum of four hours. He swore, walked briskly to the rack to get his coat, and shouted to Arthur, 'Got to rush.'

Outside it was as cold as Breughel's painted scene. He buttoned his coat as he hurried out the school and down the nearest side street. He had his keys in his hand and began clicking on the open button as he walked. Then he stopped. It was not there. His car was not there.

Damn, he thought. *It's been nicked.* He stared at the space where he had parked, now occupied by someone else's four-by-four. *Damn. This was why I left Hackney twenty years ago. To escape all this.* He began to plan his afternoon anew. He would need to call the insurance people, the police, call Head to take time off - he would need to make a statement - call Maureen, call …

But …

But there it was. Fifty yards up the road. His car. His black Golf. He marched and then began to jog across the intervening distance. Yes, that was it. Number plate, colour, scratch on the front bumper. He clicked open the door, but did not immediately get in. Instead he stood with his hand on the roof and tried to recall the morning's drive. Was his memory faulty? Had he in fact parked here, not there? He looked up and down, trying to visualise the moment of his arrival. And then a more sinister thought began to take shape. Joy riders. One of the boys. The seventeen year olds would have licences. Would they ever ... Could they ever ...

He got in the vehicle, started up, and moved off. One small mercy - he did not have a parking ticket. He hoped a place would now be free inside the school. He made a mental note to have a word with the headmaster.

Mike had been buttonholed during lunch by the school secretary Elvira Hathaway, a lady whom even Arthur Goldstone described as sepulchral.

She reminded Mike he was late with the end-of-year report cards, the completion of which he saw as a task as necessary as it was dreary, and he knew he had to use up a free period in the afternoon to finish them. Most of the reports he filled with statements which even the parents would regard as near-cliché. *Satisfactory; Must try harder; Capable; Solid.* He had learned long ago that attempts at the truth, especially for the less gifted, would mean trouble with inspectors, and were therefore to be avoided.

As he came to the card for Thomas Ephis, he paused. The boy always attained middling results in the exams, and yet occasionally, just once or twice, had demonstrated a kind of lazy brilliance. Mike remembered a class in which he had presented the formula for the sum of the first n cubes. The derivation was part of the curriculum and depended on both the sum of the first n integers and the first n squares. The calculation was laborious and took the whole lesson. At the end Ephis had approached him with an alternative proof. It was scribbled in pencil on half a sheet of paper. Mike dismissed him with a sneer. But checking during lunch he had been astonished to find it was correct. And, moreover, demonstrated a new and startling insight.

He assumed the boy copied it from the internet, but that evening, as he surfed, he could not find the proof anywhere on the standard websites.

The Evil Genius

For the boy's report he had written, *Shows potential*. He now took out his pen and for a moment considered crossing it out and replacing it. But with what? *There is a real talent there, if only ...* If only - what? ... he worked harder? ... he took an interest? Of course, if the boy had in fact cribbed the result after all, Mike would look gullible and foolish.

He put his pen away and took the Christmas card out of his pocket. The Breughel continued to trouble him in a way that he could not pin down. The snow. The frozen lake, a winter of a severity we did not suffer in the modern era. The menace of the hunters with their dogs and their weapons as they looked down at the village. Just what were they hunting? The villagers themselves?

He opened the card. Lines of signatures.

    Tom Ephis
    Tom Ephis
    Tom Ephis

And what did the boy mean? Hadn't there been two lines, not three? He tried to remember Arthur's words - *He's signed it more than once.*

Mike rubbed his eyes.

He did manage to leave while it was still light. He stopped at the shops to buy bread and milk, suspecting that his wife may not have been out.

He was right. She sat on the sofa in her dressing gown reading.

He kissed her on the forehead - she barely reacted - and then laid his things on the kitchen table. When she was like this he knew it was better to say little. He set about preparing supper.

Later they watched the news. She smoked two cigarettes.

As they prepared to retire she said to him, 'I'm so looking forward to hearing from Mum and Dad over Christmas.' He looked at her. 'I do wonder what they've been up to,' she said.

'Now Maureen …' he sighed. 'You mustn't …'

She had of late re-embraced the Catholicism in which she had been brought up. She now went to mass regularly. Some weeks it was the only time she stepped out of the house. The priest sometimes came afternoons to visit. Mike had expressed concern that there was a danger of blurring the afterlife with the here-and-now. The priest told Mike not to worry. *She may sound as if she's communing with her dead parents on a daily basis,* he said. *That's just part of the grieving process. It'll pass.*

'What do you think they would like for Christmas?' she said to him as they prepared for bed. 'It's not long now.'

And then she pulled back the covers and got in on his side.

'Maureen.'

As long as they had been married, he had slept on the right side of the bed, she on the left.

'What are you doing?' His voice, he realised, was raised. She stared at him. 'That's my side. Look. My things are there. My …'

'Yes?'

He looked at the bedside tables to the left and right. 'What?' His book, his alarm clock, the case for his reading glasses. All on the other side. 'Have you moved everything?'

'Oh stop fussing,' she said.

He stood, mouth open. *It'll pass*, the priest had said. Mike walked round to his wife's left and got into bed.

He got up early. Twice during the night he had awoken suddenly when he almost slipped off the bed.

He dressed, made himself an instant coffee. Last day at school. Lessons finished at lunch. A beer at the pub on the Headmaster's tab, then home by three.

He was out of the house by eight-fifteen.

It had snowed overnight and traffic was slow. He began to plan the lessons that were scheduled. With the upper fifth he could repeat his class of the previous day. He might tie in *The Hitchhiker's Guide to the Galaxy*. Why had this not occurred to him before? What was that joke, the answer to Life, The Universe and Everything? Forty-nine?

Or would all this be too old-hat for his pupils?

Perhaps, more perversely, might they fancy a touch of the bizarre. The Inca concept of the afterworld, interleaving with our own. Or the Hindu doctrine of Maya, the universe reduced to illusion. Or the Buddhist Void.

He shivered. It suddenly seemed too close to the melancholy and delusory state his wife was trapped in.

He switched on the radio. The car ahead slowed and then stopped. Mike craned his neck. Fifty yards away there were roadworks and a diversion. When the traffic began to move once more he followed the line of cars off down a side road to the right, and then left, right, right again, a series of sharp turns. Once the line stopped. Then zigzagged forward once more. More turns. *This can't this be right.* And then quite suddenly he was back. Right back where he had started. *Whoa, what's happening?* He was waiting at a temporary traffic lights on red, with a diversion sign ahead of him.

He swore. He had done a full circle. Worse, he should have realised earlier in this merry-go-round that he was going nowhere. He had lived here for twenty years, he knew these streets.

Once more he followed the traffic as it led him off the main road. He counted off the turnings, looking for the point where he had made his error last time round. Two, three, four, five … Six, seven …

His engine had stalled. He was staring straight ahead. A horn sounded continuously behind him.

He was back to square one. Square one. Back at his starting point.

He wound down the window and called over a workman. The man wore day-glo, a helmet. He carried a shovel.

'Excuse me, just what's going on?'

'Diversion.'

'Yes. So, what's going on?'
'You what?'
'What's happening?'
'You what?'
'Say something.'
'You what?'
'Is this a joke?'
The man made an obscene gesture.

Mike watched him walk away. The car behind him was honking again. He pulled once more to the right, but this time he left the line of traffic as soon as he could. He knew the geography around here, and, as soon as he saw a road which was not blocked and which led him roughly where he wanted to go, he turned onto it. He counted the next streets off in his mind - *Acacia Avenue, Portcullis Drive, Churchill Road, Wellington, Nelson,* ... as if by sheer will he could impose his mental map on the actual world.

At half-past-nine he saw the school ahead of him. He swore again. Nine-thirty. Someone, he hoped, would have kept an eye on his class. He hoped also that today there was a free parking space.

As he approached, he guessed that at least his second wish would be fulfilled. There were no other cars by the entrance, nor were there any on the pathway into the school. And nor in the car park itself. His was the only vehicle. He swept into the space by the main door, switched off the engine, and gazed around him. His sense of urgency dissipated. Where was everyone? Had they all been scared off by the snow?

He got out of the car, locked it and walked into the school. It was silent. The buildings were dark and cold. His shoes echoed as he made his way to his own class. He leaned against the door. The room was locked. He twisted the door handle a couple of times, waiting for the lock to give, and banged the palm of his hand against the panes of glass in the doorframe.

The Evil Genius

Once he shouted out, *Hello*. Pointlessly. There was no one inside or out.

He walked back to the entrance to the hall, stepped outside and once again shouted. *Hello, Hello*. His voice echoed. And then at the side of the building he saw one light on. The school secretary. Her office. If anyone could provide some sense and sanity, some continuity, it was her.

He hurried back inside at a jog, went up the stairs to the third floor. He opened the door of her office without knocking. 'What's going on?' he shouted. And then he stared.

Elvira Hathaway sat at her desk. She looked up at him, her eyes and mouth wide open. A pinkish blonde mountain of hair sat on top of her head. 'Elvira, what is that? Your …' He stopped himself. 'What's going on,' he said more softly. 'Your hair …' Had she been grey, Victorian in style, even twenty years ago when he had joined the school? Surely. He tried to recall her as she was just the previous day. A bun, severe, it's colour monochrome.

He had to say something. 'Your hair. It looks …' Ridiculous, he did not say. '… remarkable.'

'Mr. Wallis,' she said. 'What are you doing here?'

'Where is everyone? Where's my class?'

'Where? At home, I would have thought.'

'Why aren't they in school?'

'In holiday time?'

'But we break up today. Today. At one.'

She looked at him. He could not stop staring at her hair.

'There's one more day.'

'Mr. Wallis. You know very well we packed them off yesterday. I'm just here to tidy up.'

'I …'

He sat down on a hardbacked chair by the door.

'Mr. Wallis, are you all right?' Elvira got out from behind the desk and walked over. She wore a polka-dot mini-skirt and knee-high leather boots. Miss Hathaway. Her very name suggested a gothic novel.

He began to find it difficult to look her directly in the eyes. 'It's OK,' he muttered, and got up and left the room, walked slowly down the stairs, along the corridor and through the main door. He climbed into his car, put his key in the ignition, but did not start up. He remained in his seat.

He wanted to call someone. But who? His wife, she would still be in bed. Besides, she was nuts. No. His dear wife, what was he saying. Not nuts. No, no.

Arthur? Sarcastic, sneering Arthur?

He saw the card. On the driver's seat. The detail from Breughel. There was something about that card. About that boy.

He opened it. The boy's name. The signature. How many times had he written it?

It was splattered across the bottom of the inside page.

Tom Ephis Tom Ephis Tom Ephis Tom Ephis Tom Ephis Tom Ephis Tom Ephis Tom Ephis Tom Ephis Tom Ephis Tom Ephis Tom Ephis Tom Ephis

He stared. At the words running into each other. At the words running into each other.

In one movement, he put the card down, turned, barged open the door, and sprang out the vehicle. He ran back into the school, up the flights of stairs, into Elvira's office. She stood by a filing cabinet. The same absurd beehive, the same boots.

'Mr. Wallis. You're back,' she said. 'I'm just about to close up.'

'Elvira, I need an answer.'

'To what?'

'I must get an address. A phone number.'

'For whom?'

'One of my boys. Thomas Ephis.'

'Ephis? I don't think we have anyone by ...'

'He's in my class.'

'Are you certain?'

'I assure you …'

'I can't give you his number. Even if you're right. Only the head …'

But Mike had slid into her chair and taken hold of the mouse of her computer.

'Come on, it's here. Somewhere. The register.'

'Mr. Wallis.' She coughed. 'Mr. Wallis, you can't do that.' She approached the table.

'Elvira, please.' He clicked open a directory, scanned the spreadsheets. 'I need his number. I need the answer to an important question. I'm sorry. It's urgent.'

'Mr. Wallis, you can't …'

His eyes moved down the list of files. IIa, IIb, IIIa, IIIb, …. Va, Vb, l-VIa ..

'l-VIa. Is that Lower Sixth? Elvira?' He opened the file without waiting for a reply. There was a list of names. He scrolled down. Dawson, J. Dravid, S. Dunton, H. Eaves, M. Farringdon, J.

'No,' he shouted. 'No. No. No. Where is he?'

'Where is who?'

He saw a file marked SchoolRoll.xls. Every class. Every pupil.

'Mr. Wallis, you have to leave. Now.'

He opened it. Scrolled down. Scanned. Emmerton, D. Ennis, M. Epo, K. Epps, J. Epstein, B.

E's. E's. There must be more. Somewhere.

'Mr. Wallis.'

Somewhere.

'Mr. Wallis.'

His fingers paused at the keyboard and then lay still. Elvira Hathaway watched and waited. After a while he clicked the spreadsheet shut, got up from the chair and, without looking at her, shuffled over to the window. There was silence in the room. He stared out at the scene below. The sky was clear, but the snow on the ground remained thick. It covered the car park, the road, the trees in the distance, the open land in front. But there was no sign of goalposts or the football field that should have been there. Instead he could see the outline of a pond, its surface covered in ice. It was beautiful, he thought. And in that beauty there lay a new terror.

He turned towards the door. Elvira had backed away into a corner. She held a pair of scissors in her hand. He moved in a wide arc across the room and left. He heard the door slam behind him.

It was dark as he felt his way down the stairs, but he was caught by the intensity of the light in the car park outside. It did not surprise him that a black Toyota, his car, still the only vehicle, stood two places down. He looked through the windscreen. The Christmas card was lying folded on the driver's seat. He did not dare open up to look at it again.

He walked across the snow right up to the edge of the pond. It seemed to extend to the far horizon. He heard horns. Dogs barking. Hunting horns. In his imagination, some imagined world?

He placed one foot cautiously on the ice surface of the pond. A window opened behind him and he turned to look. A single frame of light against a darkening brick background. Someone - something, goggle-eyed, grotesque, barely human - stood at the window frame, leaning out and crying, 'Mr. Wallis, don't go there, it's dangerous …' He brought his other foot forward.

And then in the distance, at the centre of the lake, he saw a crouched figure with its back to him. Grey boots, dark trousers, grey hoodie, the face turned away. As he strained his eyes he saw the figure was sitting on a small stool in front of a

The Evil Genius

discolouration, a blob of greyish black. A circular hole in the ice, he realised as he stared. As if the figure was fishing.

He began to move forward, one careful step after the other.

A shriek behind him. 'The ice will break.'

But the world at his back made no sense any more and he carried on walking. And as he moved, the ice surrounding him lost its sheen and became in an instant grey and opaque and it seemed to him as if it could never have been anything other than grey and opaque, and its murkiness was reflected in the sky above and the sky itself seemed to dim.

After a while he stopped and looked around and over the ashen layer of ice which stretched away. In the middle distance the figure squatted and stared into the depths beneath the hole. And then a crack appeared directly between him and the stranger. It spread, slowly, zigzag, across the ice that separated them, and Mike felt his balance waver and the surface of the world tip, as if there were unplumbed liquid depths below. He thought to cry out to the stranger, who remained still, unperturbed by the breaking ice, but his courage failed him.

A horn sounded once more, this time closer. He teetered on the ice, and as he lurched he recalled the question for which he had craved an answer just minutes before.

But as he looked down at the widening crack, as his world fell away, the answer to a different question came to him.

He knew that right here beneath him, at the centre of this world, or any other, he would find only nothing.

At that moment the stranger turned.

Eudaimonia

'What do you want?' he said.
'I want to be happy,' she replied. 'That's all.'
'Happiness,' he mused. 'What is that?'
'I don't know. But ...'
'You know when you've got it?'
'You know when you've lost it.'
'And once you had it?'

She thought. She remembered a young girl. Someone who delighted in the suppleness of her limbs, for whom walking, running, jumping, somersaulting, all were equally effortless. All were actions which drew an electric charge right up from the earth beneath her feet.

'Yes.'

Movement. That was the thing. Once, it had been as well to be in motion as to be still. That was what it was to be alive. That was what made living good.

'Once.'
'When did you lose it?'

'When?' She let out a sigh. 'When I began to fear the chill of the morning. When I began to stay in bed till noon. When the utter tedium of brushing my teeth became unbearable. When walking out the door and running for a bus and fighting my way through the crowds became ...'

'Became what?'

'It's as if ...' She stared beyond him. '... as if I'm neck high in treacle.'

He considered this for a while. 'So that's it?' he said.

'Yes,' she said. 'That's it.' And then, 'All I really want is this. I want to want to get up in the morning.' There was silence across the table. 'Tell me.' Her eyes met his. 'Is that so unreasonable?'

Tears

I remember the first time I heard my mother crying.

It's strange but I remember that I wasn't really frightened at the beginning. Perhaps it was because it was the first time, and when you are that age, you see things you've never seen before as, well, interesting and curious. At the very least, you want to find out a bit more. So when it happened, and I remember it was late, well past my bedtime, I just had to get up and investigate. I must have been asleep, although it's so long ago now that I can't be sure. But when I was that age, I used to nod off pretty quickly. It's not like now, when I toss and turn for ages and just can't get things out of my mind. But at that age, I didn't think about things very much, or at least I took them pretty much as they came. And that's important as well, because that's what made me want to crawl out of bed to see what was going on.

There was a banister which ran alongside the stairs down to the ground where the living room and the kitchen were, and when the bedroom light was off, I used to slither down the steps holding on to the white slats. I thought I was being invisible. That's what I thought. I was pretty small then, and as long as I hid my eyes behind the wooden posts so that I could not see the others, well, it seemed to me, they couldn't see me.

So when I heard this strange sound, I slid down in my pyjamas and stopped about halfway. I remember I just sat there for ages and ages, while I tried to figure out what the sound was. The door of the kitchen was slightly open, and there was a light inside. I heard my father talking, I couldn't quite hear what he was saying, but then he stopped, and the noise started up again. It was a strange *gulping* sound. That's the only way I can describe it. Like an animal trying to eat something. And then a high-pitched hiccup. Which happened twice, or three times, very quickly. One after the other. Or that's what I thought. I know I sat there wondering whether my mother and father had brought someone, or some*thing*, home with them. I was excited. I always wanted a pet. A dog, or a cat. Or even a hamster like my friend Daphne. And then suddenly I knew who it was. There was no one else there. It was my mother making these odd sounds.

At that moment I realised something else. I was pretty thick then. I know. It took a while to sink in. But I knew that she was making the same noise as I made when I scraped my elbow on the concrete playground, or when I had that argument with my father after he didn't let me stay up to watch the football. But the sound was different as well. It was worse. As if she had not just scraped her elbow, but her legs and arms and her tummy. I was scared then. Really scared.

I don't know how it ended. Whether I crawled back upstairs to my room. Maybe I fell asleep on the stairs, and my father found me like that and carried me back to bed.

I do remember that things seemed to change from that night on.

For a start it happened again soon after, and then again once more. Pretty soon it became a regular thing. She sat in her chair, and rubbed her eyes with a tissue, while my father stood by and tried to say things. But it didn't help. And he seemed, well, pretty useless when you think about it. And that shocked me. Because I always thought that there was nothing he couldn't do, if he really put his mind to it. But he looked small, much smaller than he had ever seemed before.

There was something else, though. Which was that my parents ignored me while it was going on. I mean, sometimes I actually wanted to be ignored. When I was on the beach looking

Tears

for crabs, or playing with Daphne and Tom in the park. I wanted to stay out forever. I hated it when they came looking for me. But this was different. I could be hungry, or perhaps I needed help with my sums. I wanted to be noticed, but it didn't matter, it was as if I did not exist. And when they were like this I was too frightened to speak up.

One day – it must have been months later, months after I first heard that sound from the stairway – something else happened which seemed to make everything worse. It started out like it had every other time. The three of us were at the table having our tea. And then, like something creeping up out of the blue, she was crying again. This time, though, she began to scream. Loud, at the top of her voice. And she shook her head. I mean, really shook it hard. As if she wanted to just shake something right out of her mind. Like it had been hurting her all day. And then my father just ran out of the house. He ran. Like I do when I'm rushing for the school bus.

I wanted to crawl behind the curtains. But I did not move. I just stared, until eventually she began to sob, and then seemed to fall asleep. It seems kind of weird. But that's what she did. It was just for a moment though. She woke up, and grabbed me and held me so tight I could not breathe. I was too afraid to struggle.

My father did not come back for a week.

Genghis Khan

Tomorrow will be difficult, Ellie thought.

She sat at her desk, the phone in her left hand. A diary lay spread open in front of her, the tips of its upper corners indistinct, almost greyed out beyond the pool of light from the spot. *What could I cancel?...* She ran the middle finger of her free hand down the right-most page, pausing at each appointment. *... if I really had to?* Her glance flickered over the handset, and its display lit up as her thumb brushed the keypad, but the fingers of her other hand stayed put, the oily texture of the paper quite suddenly agreeable and warm under the skin.

She put the phone down and began to leaf through the pages for the coming days and weeks, the entries sparser, more speculatively hedged with queries and pencilled alternatives as April and then May stretched ahead. But it seemed as if these hooks from the future muddied rather than clarified her sense of present necessity.

Silence.

She sighed. *I wonder ... whether this one will be my last.* She had kept them, her appointments diaries, the last fifteen, twenty years. A life in print. They stood upright, arrayed and in sequence, on a high shelf somewhere above her. But her friends were all using these new hand-held gizmos these days. No more paper. Gone, the visible weight of the past. A different sense of the momentum of time, of the pull of the future.

Right. Now. Call her, let's do it ...

But she didn't. 'Aigh.' She cried out as the front door rattled. Creaking, downstairs, a key still twisting as the door swung open. She clenched her fists, the male presence, even at a distance, finally puncturing her indecision.

She took a breath and shouted at the wall. 'Darling?'

Something, his bag, tossed onto the floor. Letters ripped open, heavy footfalls, and then, as she turned, Bernard's face at the door.

'You're busy?' His voice a whisper.

'A few more minutes.'

His eyes narrowed slightly, just as they did when he bent to kiss her, and then he was gone.

She stared at the wall for a second, closed the diary and picked up the phone again. This time she dialled straight away.

'Hello?'

'Susan. It's me.' A deep breath. 'How're things?' And then, 'Been busy?' But immediately she tensed, and a shiver of embarrassment ran through her. At the subtle challenge in the question. As if her friend might have been in bed all day.

Perhaps Susan felt it as well. 'It's been hectic. I was in at eight.' And she spoke about her schedule. The minutiae of her dealings with judges, with clerks, with social workers. An obstructive barrister, a slippery client. But Ellie was glad to let Susan talk. Ellie's shoulder muscles, tight and hunched, began to loosen.

'Tell me about it,' she said as Susan appeared to stumble and run out of steam. 'So. Are we OK for tomorrow evening?'

A pause. 'It's very sweet of you ...'

'Around seven?'

'Ellie. I'm just not sure.'

'Simon?'

'He's in Frankfurt.'

'Frankfurt?'

'You know. His job.'

Ellie frowned. 'Just for an hour or two?'

'It's just that …'

Ellie waited. Then she said, 'Are you alone tomorrow?'

'I just want to … '

'Susan ...'

'I just might, well, go visit Francis.'

'Susan, are you alone?'

'I just want to walk amongst the … perhaps lay some flowers … You know, tomorrow will be exactly a year.'

One whole year.

'To the day,' Susan said.

'I know.'

'Though this time, there won't be all those people, those reporters, the police … at least I hope so … although you can never tell, they get up to such tricks … or so my friend says, the one who works at the *Guardian* … I suppose they have to, don't they, it's their job, if they don't do it, someone else will, it's dog-eat-dog, I suppose, it's … it's ...'

Ellie listened, and in the silence imagined her friend, eyes suddenly closed, mouth clamped shut, fists clenched, willing herself not to let a squeak past, not the tiniest squeak. And she knew that Susan was right, there would be no reporters, it was old news, there were other horrors occurring every day, on the tube, in the pubs and clubs, amongst the needles and used condoms of the estate which separated her own street, with its BMWs and its tennis court, from the fortified private school to which her neighbours sent their children. 'What time?' she said calmly, evenly. 'Susan, tell me, what time are you going to the cemetery?'

'Oh, Ellie.' The voice high, almost shrill. 'I couldn't impose. I won't.'

And Ellie felt herself impelled to reach over and switch off the desk-lamp. 'Susan, don't be silly. Of course I'm free.' As if to hide. As if her pretence, this lie about her workload the next day, would in the darkness be somehow more convincing. 'I'm free all afternoon.' Her voice steady in the darkness. Soothing. 'Two o'clock, how does that sound. I'll be there. OK? Susan?'

After a minute, she switched the light back on, stood, and looked about her. There was a bottle of water around. Somewhere. She reached up and along the shelves above, paused, swore, and then, her attention diverted, pulled down a slim, leather-bound book. She cradled it in her hands, opened it at the last page. She almost smiled. Every year, the same damn book. The same size, the same shade of black. The organisation of the days, the weekends, the bank holidays. And like this year's diary, every day filled with its dry recitation of the markers which staked out the landscape of her existence. Appointments, plane flights, speaking engagements, drinks parties. And yet, moving backwards through the months, stopping occasionally at an event which she had forgotten, she knew last year's diary was different from every other. Not because of what it contained, but instead because of what it did not.

She flipped the pages, back, further back. Eleven months to the day, then three weeks more. Five days, six, seven ... Strange days. Blank days. A meeting, pencilled in, with ... with someone. Who? An entry never completed. Who could it have been? A pause in the flow. And, forward from there, nothing. Nothing. For a whole week.

A hiatus. A gap. Were anyone ever to reconstruct her life, this life of hers, they would find a strange period just here where nothing, nothing whatsoever, seemed to happen.

A death.

Of sorts.

A period of no history.

They lay in bed.

'Simon's such a schmuck,' Ellie said.

Bernard nestled his face between her chin and shoulder. His middle finger traced circles over her stomach. She placed her hand over his.

'I'm putting on weight,' she said.

'No you're not. Anyway, I like it.'

'Did you make the appointment?'

'The clinic?' He looked up. 'Next Thursday. That guy on the telly might actually be seeing us.'

'Do you really think he can help?'

'Good track record.'

'You make it sound like … treating a hernia.'

'I didn't mean…. It's just… there are lots of couples like us. Who've been helped by his …'

'Hmm.' She breathed in. 'I wish …'

'What?'

'Sometimes, I wish …'

She loved it that he knew when to wait. 'I wish that I'd known you twenty years ago.'

He chuckled. 'The past's gone.'

'It's just …'

'What?'

'If we do … fingers crossed …'

'Yes?'

'We'll be old when they're still at school.'

'So? That's not unusual these days.'

She kissed the top of his head.

'You still nervous about it?' he said.

'I don't know.'

He drew her close.

'I just don't know,' she said.

*

'We estimate that about a million people died when the armies of Genghis Khan swept through Persia …'

Ellen Parson lectures at a central London university college. She teaches mediaeval history. She has always loved her job.

'… A million people. In the space of two years.'

She dresses the part. She has come to treasure the tension and the discipline of the lecture hall. She is immersed in the sense that she has inherited the rights to an ancient and complex ritual of give and take. Her students' keenness and innocence for her wisdom. A continuity and a bond. The strange intangibles of her job. There is something inspiring in them. Almost mystical.

'Recall that this war was fought, as it were, on a whim …'

She disdains the deliberately ragged demeanour favoured by some of her colleagues. Her black trouser suits, her carefully bobbed hair, even her frequent visits to the gym, all confer, it seems to her, a respect and a focus in her students' eyes, a focus which underpins this ritual.

'... after the Mongol armies had subdued the Chinese, ...'

She speaks without a microphone.

'... and after the Persians had snubbed the Khan ...'

But this time, it happens more frequently these days, the words feel inert, stripped of the cold, analytic flame which might light up her enthusiasm and the interest of her undergraduates. This exercise of delving into the past, of reconstructing lives, of re-imagining the shape of people's desires and achievements, an activity usually peppered with the same intensity she once felt as a teenager studying Caesar's Gallic campaigns, today feels stale. Which perhaps it is. Re-hashed. She has given the same lecture course many times over the last few years.

'... by failing to offer tribute.'

Even as she talks, her mind wanders, and she imagines what Susan will be doing this morning, what time she will be rising, what she will be selecting from her wardrobe to wear.

'We can estimate the number of dead by collating data …'

Ellen pauses at the lectern as a door opens at a level high above her. She waits without looking up, but senses, as a kind of swirl around her, a hundred bodies gawping and twisting in the tiers of seats stretching away. She studies her notes, the annotations in red pen, the amendments and crossings out. She aligns her papers against the edge of the desk, and raises her eyes. The newcomers are still fidgeting and arranging bags and pencils. She coughs before continuing.

'… from a number of sources. There are contemporary accounts, of battles and armies, with their quaintly poetic descriptions of rivers of blood …'

Ellen glances up, and surveys the young faces arrayed in front of her, their stretched adult features not yet quite masking the rounded vulnerability of the child within. Hair brutally shaved. Or else spilling over faces and notebooks. Some look directly at her, others stare at their desks, hands rubbing necks or chins.

'… but we can also look at indirect pointers, such as the dropping off of trade, the movements of refugees, even the alteration of weather patterns as farming, building, irrigation projects, are reduced or abandoned.'

She sees one particular boy in the front row, separated a foot or two from his companions. Larter. He is staring straight at her, and she finds herself wondering, even as she notices him, whether students still get crushes on lecturers, or whether, in this modern era of sexual *glasnost*, the youngsters are, all of them, already sated, sexually replete, shorn of the nuanced desire and self-doubt of previous generations of adolescents.

Larter. One of the brightest.

As was Francis, of course. He was about Larter's age. He *would have been* Larter's age. If he had been here.

'… but it is personal testimony which is most compelling.'

Larter is in one of her tutorial groups. They meet in her rooms once a week. Three girls, by turns flirty and serious. One mature student, an American. An Asian boy who never says a word but whose essays are good. And Larter. Larter sits apart. He has, it seems, feral views on personal hygiene.

'Contemporary accounts refer to the sacking of cities, and their razing by fire. Yet their destroyers did not seek booty or treasure. And if their foes surrendered before the fighting had begun, they could show mercy. Above all they were impatient, rootless. Nomadic. With one battle over they would move on to the next.'

Larter. She is disturbed by something he has said.

They had been discussing their essays, Larter's the last of the six. As she leant over to hand him his paper he had picked his nose. The girls made faces. Ellie breathed in sharply.

'Larter, …' He the only one to whom she refers by surname alone. '… quite superb.'

He did not respond.

She stared at the ink-blackened tips of his fingers as he grabbed the half-dozen sheets of paper. 'Can I …?' She leaned forward. 'Can I have a word? After we're done?'

Later, as the others collected their bags and papers, he had shuffled forward.

'You know I've been proposing students for postgrad?' she said.

'I, er, …'

'I have.'

He said nothing.

'And I've put your name forward.'

'Really?'

She waited. The others seemed to be taking their time, hanging around as if to catch what she was about to say.

'I'm not sure …' His awkwardness somehow at odds with the fluency of his essays.

'You should consider it.'

'Am I really the right kind of ...'

'Most certainly,' she said.

'I don't know.' He sighed, and put down his books.

'Sit down,' Ellie said. He remained standing and looked around the room.

'It's just that ...' He started to lower himself into the seat, but then stood again. 'I've not been ... well, feeling so good recently.' He began to talk. He said he had been working too hard. Not sleeping. Drinking too much.

She said nothing until he finished. 'You don't need to decide now. Wait till the summer break ...'

'My mum's friend is a psychiatrist.'

'I see.'

'She says it's ... well ... it's my studies.'

'Your studies?'

'It's not you,' he said quickly. 'But ... she says I should transfer out.'

'Ha,' Ellie could not stop herself. 'Isn't that a bit ... over the top?'

He spoke more, of depression, of strange fits. He said he was taking tablets. He looked up at the ceiling for a moment, shook his head, and muttered to himself. Ellie struggled to hear.

'Larter.' She broke in after a moment. 'Larter, I think you have fantastic potential. A really bright future. Larter?'

'Tell me.' He frowned and bit his lip. 'Do you still ...?'

'What?'

Now, as she pauses in front of the students and drinks from a glass of water, she tries to recall the exact words he used. He had said something about the buzz. Whether she still found it interesting. Or fulfilling. Or fun. Or something.

'What on earth do you mean?' she replied. She remembers that.

'All this.' He waved his sheaf of papers, and then pointed at the books piled onto shelves around them. 'Do you still like doing it?'

'Why ...' She reddened. 'Yes. Yes, I do.'

'Even after ...'

'Even after teaching for, how many years is it now ...? Yes. I'm never bored.'

He rubbed a finger against his cheek, the corner of his mouth, the bridge of his nose. 'I don't just mean ... getting bored.' His voice dropped a register. 'Doesn't it ever shock you? What you study? The things you teach?'

He whispered. He said he had become obsessed by something. By something in the history she taught. He thought about it all the time. 'It's the ... the sheer carnage,' he said. The carnage. Its scale. Its magnitude. He said he was haunted by the men they studied, these empire builders, dictators, slave traders. By their addiction to blood and power. He said that sometimes it was the small detail that appalled. A nephew tortured, a daughter raped. The nature of the torture. The ingenuity of its cruelty. Sometimes it was the big picture. The numbers massacred, crucified, or burnt.

One of the girls, just outside the door, began to giggle.

'Doesn't it bug you? Doesn't it ... don't you ... care?'

For a few moments Ellie said nothing. She considered his words. 'Of course.' She swallowed. 'Of course I care. But caring doesn't stop us wanting to understand. Does it?'

In a sudden gesture he bared his teeth. She felt herself becoming just faintly alarmed at his distress.

'How *can* we understand?' He paused, and then he was talking again, his voice louder. He said that time and distance prevented understanding, that it was all so different here and now in the modern era, that no one he knew, no one he had ever met, had the faintest idea how to fight, or to kill, or to maim, had the faintest clue how to do these things. He stuttered, 'And that's a good thing. A good thing. Isn't it. Tell me it is.'

She said nothing for a few moments. 'And so?'

'So we can't understand them. Can we?'

'Is that really true?'

'And yet, in those days, they all knew. Every one of them. Your Mongol warriors. Every single one of them knew these things.'

It's not quite true, she thought, *What you say. Some still do know how to do these things,* and she thought of Francis, alone, one morning in the early hours, walking home. And his two assailants. A few sharp words, his bemused, semi-drunken reply, and then a knife to the flesh of his stomach. All for a phone and some loose change.

'And everything we learn, your lectures, the course books, it counts for nothing. Because we just don't really understand the scale of this ... this holocaust.'

Ellie was silent.

'We ignore it. We forget the victims. And it just seems so …'

He scratched his head, and then he was talking again. A dream he had, a recurring dream. Himself, there, on the steppes of the lowlands of Mongolia centuries before. Slaughtering, burning. There was a stifled laugh from the hallway, and for just a second Ellie succumbed as well to the image of this pale, fragile boy, astride a half-broken colt, club or dagger in hand. She remembered one of her own lectures, she recalled her own exact words, that every able-bodied man, every teenage boy, from thirteen, fourteen on, knew how to ride, how to use bow and arrow. 'At your age, most had already killed.' Those were her words. She had explained how the young men practised on animals. And then on their foes. Or even on their peers. 'Those who survived an often brutal childhood, that is.'

Larter stared at the floor. 'It just seems so … I don't know … so cheap.'

'Cheap?' Her voice rose.

'Yes. Cheap.'

Ellie looked up at the folders and notebooks scattered over her desk, the hardbacked books on her shelves, many written by men and women she knew, or admired, or loathed. One or two written by her. 'But that isn't the whole story,' she said. 'These ... these waves of humanity spreading west from the hinterlands of Asia. That's the stuff of history. Each wave brings something. Trade, or culture. Religion. Philosophy. These things are the building blocks of ... well, of what we are. Us.'

She breathed in as she spoke, desperate suddenly for someone to interrupt and back her up. But the other students had gone. There was no one there. After a while she went on. 'Gradually, over time, they imposed order. They brought Chinese science to the Arabian Gulf. Western farming methods to the East. Societies perished, but others grew. There was purpose there. And also a kind of nobility. There was a morality of war. These people invested a kind of honour in the violence they practised. There was ... there is a nobility of sorts. Somewhere.' She looked up at Larter. 'Can't you see that?'

She put the glass down.

'But there is one other aspect of the Mongol invasions which has recently generated wide interest. Even outside academic circles. Geneticists have discovered a massive prevalence in a certain chromosome in some European and Asian civilisations.'

Ellen has always been proud of her efforts to introduce a multi-disciplinary flavour to her lectures.

'All stemming from a single source. A single tribe.'

But today it seems contrived.

'With conquest came wives, concubines, harems. And an overwhelming sexual profligacy.'

She looks at the clock facing her on a far wall.

'They left a legacy of the genes.'

Ten minutes remain of the lecture, and suddenly she is nervous. *Susan*, she remembers. *I need to wrap this up.*

Genghis Khan

'Does evolutionary biology afford a more fruitful model for the study of population growth, and the rise and fall of the great empires?'

She pauses, and looks out at her audience, left to centre to right. Somehow the gesture communicates itself to the students, and immediately the focus of the lecture is broken. She watches them yawning, grinning, stretching, whispering furiously to each other.

'Gentlemen. Ladies. Next week. Read the suggested texts. We'll discuss ...'

They are already packing bags and getting up to go. *Hell*, she thinks. *I must hurry.*

*

'Margery?' She strode into her office and lay her folders down on her desk. She shouted out again. 'Hello?' She picked up her keys, her diary, a packet of paracetamol, and then walked to the door.

'Margery?' She sighed as her assistant appeared. 'Any messages?' She shrugged. Ellie walked back to the desk, grabbed her coat, and then paused. She pulled her mobile out of her bag. She leaned back, the phone at her ear, her fingers rapping against the wooden surface of the desk. After twenty seconds she punched *end-call* and threw the phone into her bag.

'Margery.' She talked as she walked out the door towards the staircase. 'Cancel the session with Professor Keane at two. Tell him ... I don't know ... Tell him, I'll call later.' She skipped down the stairs, two steps at a time. 'I'm going to be away for a few hours,' she shouted.

Traffic in the inner suburbs of north London was heavy. *Tomorrow. I'll cycle.* She grinned. *Definitely.* Bernard's journey in to Whitehall was longer than hers, and yet his travel time, negotiating cycle lanes, pedestrians, the taxi drivers, in his ankle clips and helmet, was a quarter of an hour shorter. *Oxford. That's the way it should be.* She and Susan, careering across the quad, from college to bar, from digs to lecture. On those ancient boneshakers. But then, the town was small. And the traffic, in those days, twenty-five years ago, was, like everything else, civilised and light.

Oxford.

It was she who had actually gone out with Simon first, before Susan had even met him. But his austere sparkle began to seem less brilliant as the first term of her second year drew to a close. Perhaps his capacity for affectation began to pall. Perhaps for the two of them, both grammar school girls, it was Ellie who first saw through the calculation of so many of the young men, the studied disinvolvement which so many of them took as their birthright, or their natural inheritance, their reward for being rich, clever, marked out. For being there, at Oxford.

But Susan was dazzled, and then grateful when he remembered her later in London after they had graduated. And it was as if her three years of independence, her slightly surreal voyage through this timeless world of high culture and higher education, counted for nothing as she took low grade administrative jobs, and then married and prepared to have children.

They had loved those three years, of course they had, but for Ellie the enchantment had purpose, it confirmed to her what she already suspected, that her future lay in her love affair with the past, in all its intricate and – it seemed to her then – its noble complexity. The past. When the connection between action and its consequences was defined by equations which could be understood, and whose parameters had something to do with honour, prestige and the pursuit of power. And where the muddle, regret and indecision of normal, daily life could be skimmed off and ignored.

And Simon. How tawdry was the world of hedge funds and derivatives. That so many of the brightest and best found their calling there somehow came to seem offensive to her. Frankfurt.

She recalled the conversation the previous night. He was in Frankfurt. Today. Of all days.

The roads beyond the north circular were wider. Tree-lined. The cars more expensive. Ellie pulled into the avenue where Susan and Simon kept their large and eerily empty house. She parked and wondered whether to phone ahead, but instead climbed out of the car and marched up to the front door. She knocked, waited, breathed out in relief as she heard footsteps, but it was a small, grey-haired woman wearing an apron and gloves who answered, and who replied with a Spanish accent when Ellie enquired after Susan.

The woman took off her gloves. 'I tell her you called.'

Ellie thought for a moment. 'It won't be necessary.'

The cemetery was five minutes away. Ellie knew the directions by heart. It was surrounded by a high fence, and she needed to be let in at the padlocked gate by an old man in council day-glo. She walked along the aisles quickly and carefully, and then stopped.

She observed her at a distance.

Susan knelt on the grass behind a large headstone, its light grey marble smooth and its lines clean, not yet corroded by the sun and the rain. Ellie hesitated for a few seconds, and then began to move forward. She paused, just once, to get her phone out of her handbag and to switch it off.

She came close and laid a hand on Susan's shoulder. Susan reached up and placed her own on top.

After a while Ellie knelt next to her friend, Susan's face half-hidden as her gaze swept over the rows of headstones stretching away, over the flower beds and the trees in the distance. Ellie glanced at the inscription in front of them. *Francis Spears. 1986-2005.* The gold lettering immaculate and well-kept.

They sat in a Greek café at the end of the road.

'I'm so sorry about your shoes,' Susan said. 'And your trousers, they're covered in mud.'

'A smudge.'

Susan wore jeans and trainers. A baggy sweatshirt. She had dark glasses on as they walked into the café, but after the waitress had served them, she took them off.

'I'm glad you came,' she said, and smiled thinly. She was wearing no make-up. 'I'm sorry to be so difficult.'

'When's Simon back?'

Susan took a sip from her coffee, grimaced, and shook her head. 'Did you have to cancel much?'

Ellie looked at her. She was about to ask again about Simon, and then was overcome by the intuition that he was somehow out of the picture. 'No. Nothing,' she said eventually. 'Well. One meeting with that awful professor. You know, you've met him.'

They were silent. 'Look,' Ellie said, 'if you want to stay at my place for a few days … If Simon's away for a while.' Ellie watched her friend. 'If …'

'You know.' Susan pulled a packet of tissues from her bag, but she placed them down on the table unopened. 'You know, I thought of visiting them …'

'Who …?'

'Going to the jail. Seeing what they were like. What they had become.'

Two men had been picked up a few days later. There was cctv footage. DNA evidence, hairs, saliva, found on Francis' body. The trial was short. Twice, the court had to be emptied after disturbances from the extended families of the accused. The judge recommended fifteen years before the possibility of parole.

'But then …' Susan's eyes darted. She blinked rapidly. 'But then, I couldn't. And I don't think I ever will.'

Ellie signalled to the waitress and pointed to the two cups.

'I want them, not … not just, out of my life, but more.' Susan swallowed. Her eyes were dry. Her lids drooped slightly, as if half-closing, and then they were wide again. 'Out of everyone's lives. Gone. Erased.' She looked at Ellie. 'Is that possible?'

The waitress came over and placed two more cups on the table.

'Is that bad?'

They drank their coffee.

'Am I a bad person?'

It began to cloud over, and for a while it rained. But the skies cleared later. They drove to the Heath and walked. They sat at a bench and looked over the skyscrapers of the City. Children in school uniform skipped by.

'You were right,' Susan said.

'Me?'

'It's crazy. Ever to try.'

Ellie looked at her friend, but Susan continued to stare at the distant skyline.

'It's too much of a hostage to fortune. You invest so much of … so much time, emotion, sweat. So much of … everything.'

Her voice had a hypnotic smoothness. Ellie wondered whether she was taking pills.

'And then, something absolutely outside your control takes this priceless treasure away.'

'I never said that,' Ellie said, a panic beginning to flicker somewhere in her stomach. 'I never said it was crazy.' And then she thought, *Did I? Once, long ago?* But another thought came to her. *You've never guessed, have you? About me. That I might someday desire what you had.* A panic, at her friend's assumptions, at the gulf which, quite suddenly, she saw stretched out between them. Ellie began to breathe deeply and rhythmically, but it seemed to be no help. *Please ask.* She implored her friend in silence. *Ask me now.*

But Susan said, 'You know, my great-great-grandmother had six. So the records say. It may have been more. Seven, eight. Double that number. Who knows. Six survived. The rest are forgotten. And perhaps that was the way to do it. You always have something left over. No matter how many are taken.'

Later.

'But I couldn't. After Francis. It was a difficult birth ... well, you remember. That was it. Sweet Jesus, that was it.'

*

She drives through the inner-city suburbs which lie just north of the university. Her bike remains chained up back home in the hallway, Bernard too polite to show his disappointment. Traffic moves slowly. She stares up at the sky. There has been a light shower earlier. She hums to the radio. There is a sign for road works further on. Two lanes are squeezing into one.

Ellie feels rather than hears a dull thump some distance ahead. The line of cars slows and then comes to a halt. There is a sound of breaking glass. She waits, and then cranes her neck and looks. A van two vehicles ahead blocks a clear view. She glances at her watch, and then along the side of the road ahead. There is a garage to the right. Two men in overalls appear at the entrance. Each carries a rag. One of them also carries a large-gauge spanner. The other, she sees, holds a hammer. She gazes at them for a moment, and then her attention shifts across to the row of terraces next door. Windows on the upper floors are juddering open, one after the other. Faces are appearing, two, three at each window ledge. And then, at street level, she sees a crowd of men, jostling, shoving, staring at something that is going on ahead, just out of view.

A car behind begins to sound its horn, in short bursts, and then in continuous three second blasts. A man comes striding towards them out of the crowd. He stops two cars ahead and screams.

'Shut. The. Fuck. Up.'

Ellie cannot believe what she has just heard. For a moment there is silence.

Genghis Khan

A taxi in front of her begins to reverse slowly. Just inches away from her bonnet, the driver stops, and pulls to the right. He twists round, advancing, reversing, and then eases out of the line of traffic. He u-es, and as he moves past her, he lowers his window and looks across. She mouths, *What's going on?* but he just shakes his head and accelerates forward.

Ellie watches him disappearing in her side mirror, and turns to face ahead. She clenches her fists on the steering wheel and swears. A police siren, distant, barely audible, is blowing in and out with the wind. She sees a youth in a red hoodie walking through the stopped traffic, from left to right, his face hidden. He bends and squeezes his way round bumpers. A languid finger trails the chassis of every car he passes. And then she sees another. Another youth. The same red jacket. And another. Then five more. Ten. Twenty. She stares, open-mouthed, this army of ghosts threading its way through the traffic. The crowd ahead turns to watch the youths approaching, and suddenly men are rocking back and forwards on their heels, or reaching for things in their pockets. Some stoop to pick up objects from the ground.

Two people are squaring up to each other. She can see them. They shout at the top of their voices. Faces inches apart. Eyes bulging, necks taut and knotted. One of them turns and abruptly he is running. The other, his jacket falling to the ground, flies after him in pursuit. Snarling, grasping, kicking.

And then Ellie's head twists, and she gasps. A youth, no, a boy, *a boy*, is clambering up on to her bonnet. His scarlet hood falls back. His face is empty of fear or doubt. Its young beauty is unblemished, its expression void. Ellie sees in that blankness a kind of horror. He stretches and twists, as if to see what is happening ahead. She cannot move or speak, but the boy ignores her. He stands, swaying, as if dancing, and then he leaps down to join his fellows. Ellie sits, mouth open, completely still.

A knock. At her right window. A light tapping.

'Hey, lady.'

She twists and stares. Three fingers, knuckles creased and brown. Once more, a rap on the window. An old man, glasses thick and taped together, stands close by, peering in.

'Hey, lady. There's some't going on up there.'

Police sirens now insistent and multiplying, getting closer, louder. Lurching in pitch and volume, low to high, smooth to jagged.

'Hey, lady.'

'Thank you,' Ellie says. 'Thank you.'

'Hey, lady.'

She engages gear and reverses fast. The car behind her is moving as well, and honks. She brakes, turns the wheel to the right and jerks forward. She comes within inches of breaking the old man's knees. She takes a deep breath, and closes her eyes for just an instant. She reverses again, and sees four youths watching her in her mirror. They jeer. One runs forward and kicks her bumper. She stops, judders forward and arcs round, tyres screeching, over the pavement and onto the road. One of the youths runs alongside and reaches for the door. She screams.

*

'They're waiting for you.'

Margery stood in Ellie's office. Ellie laid her bag down and nodded. 'Let me just catch my breath.'

Margery stared at her. 'Are you OK?'

Ellie nodded again.

'Do you need …'

'A coffee would be fantastic.'

'Sure.' And then, as Ellie paused at the door, 'Don't worry. I'll bring it over.'

Larter and four of the others were sitting silently in their seats.

'I'm sorry,' she said. 'Traffic.'

Genghis Khan

They sat with their pads and pencils. Bags at their feet.

'Right. Where were we?' Ellie sat down. She sighed. 'Where were we?' *I move through this world, but am not part of it*, she thought.

One of the girls was talking about an essay assignment she could not meet. Ellie's mind wandered. *I'm just not part of it.* She looked up. The three girls. The American. 'Where's Rashid?' she said. 'Amanda? Anyone?' She bent to pick up her folder, and then paused, flushed momentarily with an insight, the kind of insight she remembered she used to have as a precocious teenager, that a lack of concern for the day-to-day intricacies of the lives around her somehow lay at the root of it all. 'Does anyone have a number for him?' She looked at her five students – 'Anyone?' - and in their silence she felt the edge of hysteria. *Not now*, she thought. She knew she was about to cry. There. Then. She reached for a tissue, but drew back. She concentrated on her breathing.

'Amanda.' Her voice strained, terse. 'Carry on. Please.' Ellie remained absolutely still, moving only to reach for a coffee mug as the door opened a sliver and her secretary laid a tray on a side table.

After a while, Larter picked up his essay, and Ellie nodded for him to proceed. But he hesitated and coughed. 'Does anyone else want to …?' The American put on his glasses and reached across. He began to read Larter's text, and as he relaxed into the subject matter, his voice abruptly fell. Ellie's attention slowly fastened on to the purr of his bass. She listened, anaesthetised, and began to unwind. She found herself rediscovering – discovering - it always struck her, she realised, with the shock of the new – Larter's muscular grasp of the subject. She listened, and suddenly felt that all seemed vindicated. That her knowledge could be communicated, transmuted. That this young intelligence in front of her could, under her tutelage, become something more than the sum of the things it had been taught.

Later, when the reading was finished, she asked him to elaborate on his themes. She began – tentatively, and then for the sheer pleasure of it - to prompt and prod.

Marx? Or neo-con?

Famous men? Or the struggle of the classes?

Aquinas or Luther? Newton or Leonardo? Hitler or Stalin?

At the end of the lesson, as the girls fidgeted with their bags, she took him aside.

'I hope you're feeling better,' she said.

'Hmm.' He stared at his shoes, his manner suddenly cautious, his voice squeaky and unsure now that the tutorial was over. He frowned.

'Have you thought any more?' Ellie said. 'About what we were saying?'

He began to collect together his notes. He did not meet her eye.

'Look, I understand your doubts,' she said. 'I really do. But you have a talent. For the broad sweep. For understanding motive, purpose. For what drove those people.'

He opened up his bag and placed his things inside. His face tightened into a smirk. And then he looked up. 'Understanding, you say?'

'Yes. Yes.'

'Understanding?'

'That's what I said.'

He looked down again and shook his head.

'How many ...' He began to speak, and then stopped. He looked across at the others. They were talking amongst themselves. 'That last lecture of yours, the Mongol invasions. How many dead? How many were killed?'

Ellie noticed a tiny tremor along his right cheek. 'It's in the notes,' she said after a moment.

'*Understand*, you said?'

'Yes.' And then she said. 'Perhaps the analysing, the understanding ... Larter ... Larter, look at me. Look at me.' The other students were silent. 'Perhaps,' her voice low, 'this analysis, this codifying can ...can ...'

'Can what?'

'Perhaps it can help draw the sting.'

He stared at her. Slowly he began to shake his head. 'Not for me.'

He zipped up his bag. Suddenly everyone was moving, gathering papers, shifting chairs. 'I *am* feeling a bit better, thanks.'

He stood. 'You see, I don't want to understand them. I'm not like them. I never will be.' He began to walk towards the door. 'I'm sorry,' he said. 'I just have better things to do.' And then he nodded and left the room.

*

The three of them sat round the end of the table. Bernard reached over and poured wine into Susan's glass.

'He's away all week,' Susan said. 'Perhaps it's a good thing. I've been so busy. Simon would have been in the way.'

'You shouldn't be working this hard,' Bernard said.

Susan chuckled. 'You know, there're all so desperate. My clients. It's all so squalid. And yet …' She stared into the distance. '… they're so, I don't know, up for everything.'

Bernard looked bemused. 'What do you mean?'

'Compared to us. With our mortgages and careers,' she said. 'As long as they get their giro. And their fags. As long as they can blow a few quid on the lottery each week.'

'Different lives.' Bernard moved to refill Ellie's glass, but she placed a hand over it. 'Ellie,' he said, putting the bottle down. 'What do you think? Ellie? Are we that far apart?'

She glanced at her partner and her friend - 'What?' - and looked away. Larter. Her pupil, her star pupil, his abrupt decision to leave after graduation. It haunted her and, in some strange way, challenged her, but she had said nothing to the others. She felt she had not yet assimilated what it might mean, but it came to her now that Susan would better understand what had troubled the young man. 'You know ...' she started to say, and then, looking at her friend once more, decided against. *Not now*, she thought. *Not now*.

She changed tack. 'I wonder.' She reached across for the plates. 'Your clients. That hopelessness. Perhaps we're not so far removed. You know... ' she grunted as she stretched. 'I almost got involved in something yesterday.'

'Here, let me ...'

'It may have been on the news. An accident. On the road. A bunch of men arguing.'

The others stared at her.

'I thought there was going to be a riot,' Ellie said.

She described the old man, the hoodies, the boy on the bonnet. 'Ellie.' Bernard was sitting up in his chair. His face was red. 'Why didn't you tell me?'

'What did you do?' Susan asked.

'I got out of there. Quick as I could.'

'Damn them,' Bernard said. He got up, a stack of plates in his hands. 'Damn the lot of them,' he muttered.

He shuffled over to the kitchen. Susan and Ellie glanced at each other.

Susan reached a hand across the table.

Bernard stood with Susan's coat in his hands. 'Why don't you stay?'

'Thanks. I'll call a cab.'

'I'll drive you,' Ellie said. 'I've hardly drunk a thing.'

The sky was clear, the moon full. As they passed the cemetery, a police siren sounded behind them. Ellie slowed to let the van overtake.

'They're beautiful,' Susan said.

And they were. The lines of headstones silver, the uniformity, row after row, conferring a kind of community, a sense of shared passage.

They pulled up outside Susan's house. Ellie turned off the engine. For a moment she was not sure what to do.

'Will you be OK?' she said. She turned. Susan was staring straight ahead. The wet glisten on her cheeks as silver as that of the stone. Ellie leant over. They sat, quiet and still in the darkness. After a while Susan took a deep breath and straightened. She opened her bag, felt for something inside, and then sat staring into her lap.

'I've been thinking of quitting my job,' she said.

Ellie waited a few seconds and then spoke. 'Why?'

'It's just ... I'm finding it more and more difficult ...'

'What would you do?'

'I don't know. Go abroad for a while ...'

You can't always run away... The phrase rolled around in Ellie's mind. Quite abruptly she was glad she had not said it.

'It's just ... when I see my clients ...' Susan paused for a second. 'You know I ... I sort out their legal problems. Housing benefit, immigration papers, the rest of it. I'm a kind of social worker. A mother hen. I tell them what to do. How to play the system.

'Usually it's the women. But sometimes, just sometimes, I see their husbands, their useless teenage sons. And ...'

There were footsteps in the street. A man in a suit, his tie half undone, steadied himself against a lamppost. Ellie wondered whether he was going to piss. In front of them. They waited as he stumbled past.

'The two young men who did this ...' Susan's voice was low, steady. 'Who did this thing. This thing to Francis.

'I've tried. God knows, I've tried. But I can't ... I just can't find it in me to forgive. And I don't think I ever will.

'Once, months ago, I thought of going there. To the prison. I rang the office, even made an appointment. I booked a cab. But ... it never ...'

Susan groped for the door handle.

'So now I blame them all. If they tell me their boy's in for joy-riding, or hubby's been done for drunk-and-disorderly, I ... I no longer know what to say.' Susan laughed softly. 'I no longer care.'

'I'll walk you to the door,' Ellie said.

'No. I'm fine.' And then Susan turned. 'You know, you're the only one left,' she said. 'Francis. Simon. My job. All going, all gone. It's just you and me.' She pulled on the handle and the door opened. Her eyes, whites bright and imploring in the shadow, remained on Ellie's as she climbed out of the car. For a second she stood, and then she turned and walked up to the front door of her house.

Ellie watched her friend. When Susan was inside she switched on the engine. She looked over her shoulder and began to turn, but changed her mind and decided to drive straight on. After a few minutes she saw a sign for the motorway and the north. She continued on. Half an hour later she pulled in to a service station for a coffee.

There was a message on her mobile, and she reached down for it, but then turned it off.

She sat at a plastic table and drank from a paper mug, under lights which seemed to strip away all colour.

She remembered a day twenty-five years before. A different table, a long table, a room with a high wooden ceiling. Forty young women sitting down to eat. The conversation fluid and quick, accents southern, cut-glass, neutral. A few Scottish voices. An eagerness in their chatter, an impatience. Just one girl quiet, sitting opposite Ellie, one girl on her own, glancing around the room, the glaze of her mother's nurture and love still fresh in her face. Ellie saw her look down at the table, at the array of glass and cutlery below her, the heavy, polished silver, the crystal tumblers bulbous or fluted. An array whose multiplicity of function lay beyond her. She saw the panic in the girl's eyes. As the soup was served, Ellie, her fingers practised, casual, reached for her outermost spoon. She smiled as Susan looked up, her glance for a second flickering over Ellie's right hand.

'Hi. My name's Ellen. Though everyone at home calls me Ellie.'

It began to rain as she drove back down the motorway. Three lanes of traffic, heavy despite the late hour. The illuminated city ahead of her, under a mass of grey-yellow cloud. She thought. She remembered another day, a different Susan. At the hospital, just one hour after Ellie had received a frantic call from her husband. Flowers, cards. Simon standing on tiptoe, looking sheepish.

'Have you settled on a name?' Ellie asked her.

'Just a few thousand,' Susan said, her hair still tight to the skin with the exertion and the sweat. 'What do you think?' A kind of triumph in her face, a very private triumph, as she looked down at the baby in her arms. 'Tell me, Ellie, what do you think?' she said softly.

Ellie leaned over mother and baby. 'I think he's a ...' As if to puncture that privacy. '... a John. Or a Jacob. Or perhaps ... a Francis?' Or to let it enfold her as well.

'Francis,' Susan said, and looked up. 'I like that. Francis.'

Signs ahead, ring roads, junctions. The northern suburbs. Ellie's thoughts moved forward, and she imagined herself, for the first time, for the very first time, in a similar bed, one year on, the same exhaustion and exhilaration on her face. Bernard, his parents, her mother all standing by as a nurse passed her the baby.

You're the only one left.

Her friends, her close friends beside her. *It will destroy her*, Ellie thought. This image whose possibility was shared with no one but Bernard. An image which, she realised now, she had hardly come to terms with herself. *Why didn't I tell Susan?* she wondered. But she knew the answer. She knew it was an image that she could never reveal to her closest friend. *It will kill her.* And that, when – if – the image became reality, there would be someone, her closest friend, someone so dear to her, absent from that bedside.

The image burnt inside her as she drove, and then flared, sputtered and began to fade. She thought of Bernard, she knew she ought to stop and call, that he would be worried. She remembered the appointment that he had made, at the clinic, for next Thursday. And as she crossed the north circular road on the edge of London, this fragile image in her mind, this new kind of future, the breaking of one set of ties, the building of another, this image flickered and finally died.

Next Thursday, she remembered. *I'm seeing Professor Keane. About Larter, about persuading him to stay. I almost forgot.*

She would have to tell Bernard. She wouldn't make it to the clinic. She couldn't. Not next Thursday.

And if Bernard asked her when she could make it, she would tell him, well, she just wasn't really able to plan that far ahead into the future.

After all. The future, it just wasn't her thing.

Eudaimonia

An unfamiliar bed. Unfamiliar sounds outside. Some of the hotel guests are still partying in the grounds.

A familiar body next to hers, in worn and familiar pyjamas.

'Do you think she'll be happy?' she says.

Light snores, but she knows he is still awake and nudges him in the chest.

'I'm asleep,' he says.

'Do you?' He says nothing.

She lies on her back, looking for shadows, and then sighs.

The Writers' Group

Mary

'Fuck.'
She looked at the fingers of her right hand. The middle nail was broken. And she did not wear her nails too long anyway. And - and - she still sometimes bit them. She sat down on the bed and wondered where she had left her nail file, and swore again.

'Ron,' she shouted. 'Ron, I've got to go. Group's meeting in half an hour. Ron?'

His head appeared round the door. 'What time you back?'

'Usual. Ten, ten-thirty.'

'You pubbing afterwards?'

'Come along. If you fancy it.'

'You kidding? With that lot?'

'Fuck you.'

She got up, reached for her coat, sat down again and pulled her satchel towards her. She checked to make sure she had her notes, her sketches and short stories. And Peter's submission. 'Fuck.' She had only read the first page. She'd have to bluff the rest.

'You eaten?' Ron's voice quiet then loud, as if he had just opened the toilet door.

'No.' She was shouting. 'You?'

'Take out later?'

'Sure.'

'As long as it's not curry.'

'What's wrong with curry?'

'What's it with these Brits? Can't they think of something which is not spiced up stodge?'

'When in Rome …'

'Come on. You agree with me on this.'

'No I don't.'

'Mary, you do.'

'Fuck you.'

She chuckled. Of course Ron was right. Her friends in New York had managed, just before she was transferred over here, to persuade her that the food in England was improved out of all recognition. Now, a year on, she sometimes dreamed of taking them all, each and every goddam one of them, around some of the dives she'd been to. And these places were expensive as hell.

She abandoned her search for the nail file. 'I'm out of here.'

'Later.'

As she waited for the tube she wondered how long Ron would be able to bear it in London. They had set themselves three years, and at first they could not quite believe their luck. Both their employers, his ad agency, her commodity trading company, had been enthusiastic and had smoothed away difficulties with visas. But it was clear Ron missed life back home. He just could not fit in. He described, to anyone who would listen, an incident in the lift at the block of flats in Chalk Farm into which they had moved. There were four concierges working in rotation at the front door. He had asked one of the other residents, as they entered the lift together, what their names were.

'Some stuck-up Brit,' he would relate, even if the audience was itself English. 'He didn't have the faintest clue.'

'Perhaps he'd just moved in,' she had countered the first time he told the story. 'Like us.'

'Christ, he'd been there for five years. He told me on the way up.'

'Well, so what?'

'It's that fucking class system of theirs -' a phony accent '- *one doesn't converse with the servants.*'

She laughed as she remembered it, and yet had begun, the last few weeks or so, to have the tiniest inkling that Ron was about to bail. That he was going to tell his boss it was not working and he wanted out. And if that happened it would leave her with a dilemma. A big, big dilemma. She loved her job. She had her friends, they went to the theatre, to gigs.

She had her writers' group.

Her novel.

And she did not want to give these things up.

'How do you get it so spot on?' someone at a party asked her once. They had all been drunk and were parroting favourite sections from Fawlty Towers. 'You understand us so well.' But the truth was that the very thing that drove Ron so mad, this thing that was not simply class, that both of them were clever enough to realise was a sophistication of social interaction which was based on a whole range of unspoken nuances of culture, this thing was the very quirk of life that fascinated her. And which she strove to reproduce in her fiction. She did not think she did get it spot on. But she did observe.

Like now, on the train. The kid opposite her with his bling and his legs spread wide, his hands covering his crotch. But what she found riveting was the middle-aged woman next to him with her face in a book, her body angled uncomfortably away from him, and the subtly broadcast horror on her face whenever she looked up.

Mary had started her book five years ago, the summer after her uncle died. She spent a few weekends sorting though his letters and papers, and it came to her, quickly. The story - his story - of an American airman stationed in Tokyo just after the war. The clash of old and new, vanquished and victor. His uncle had met a girl, she wasn't even named. But it had not worked out and he had returned home.

She knew she had a narrative, she had characters. She went to evening classes, dug up her old college notes on creative writing. But a year on it was not working. She struggled to find time for it, yeah, for sure, it was difficult to balance work and play. And of course she had got married. But there was another reason. The Japanese characters in her book were bland, static, wedged close all round by cliché. The post-war clash of culture - not a clash of weapons but more one of , of what?, of status, of role, of social mobility - seemed in her prose to be wooden and unconvincing.

She picked up the narrative two years later when she arrived in London. And suddenly the way forward was clear. It was the way people said one thing and meant another. It was the surface politeness and the concealed hostility. To one's social inferiors, the taxi driver, the newsagent, the concierge. And, yes, especially to the Indian waiters at the local curry house. Race. Class. Japanese or British. Here, two continents away, she could see how this Tokyo girl, her family, her peers, her society, might have resisted and finally repelled the brash flight lieutenant from Brooklyn.

Jane

Jane had not dared to read beyond the first two chapters.

It had been struggle enough to buy the book, and then to open it and start reading. And the first ten pages had not been encouraging. The prose was rather too terse for her taste, the characters were, if not two dimensional, what one nevertheless imagined most ordinary and uninformed members of the public might assume was the typical client list for a practising psychoanalyst. And the swearing. The swearing was simply unnecessary.

The Writers' Group

There were positives. The description of the first floor consulting rooms - with their views over the square, the shelves of reference works, the discreetly framed degrees and qualifications, the relative positions of desk and couch - this was disarmingly accurate, as if the author had stolen into her own rooms by night with measuring tape and camera in hand.

But more disturbing was the thought that her project, assuming it ever reached completion and got accepted by a publisher, might somehow be tarnished by comparison with the book she was holding in her hands. This book, the first piece of fiction by a grotesquely undertalented TV doctor, dwelt on the struggles of a disparate group of adulterers and alcoholics and pill-poppers as their stories found their locus and common ground in the offices of a Harley Street psychiatrist.

Her own novel, based not, categorically not, on her actual patients, but whose narrative arc would of course be informed by the experience of her own practice, could and would be better written and, if the phrase had any meaning at all, truer to life. But necessarily it would lack the selling power, the media clout of the name spelt out, in bright red italics, on the book cover she now held.

She had been minded to ask the group, the last couple of times they all met, whether any of them had read it. Or, putting the matter more precisely, she was minutely disappointed that not one of them had brought up the subject. They knew she worked as a psychotherapist, they knew that that was what she wished to write about. And they knew, god knows it had been advertised enough in the *Guardian* and *The Times*, that her literary rival's book was out. Could not at least one of them have made the connection?

By the way, did you see that A_____ C_____ has written a book just like yours?

Perhaps it was the kind of thing that was discussed in the pub afterwards rather than in the meetings themselves.

But she disliked pubs. She hardly drank these days, just the odd glass of claret. And pubs - as far as she knew - were not very good on wine. But more important was that she disliked travelling on the tube late at night. Far better to sit quietly, at a reasonable hour, on the Bakerloo line, and just hope that those brutish youths did not have their personal stereos on too loud. And she would be back in time to watch the late news with a biscuit and a cup of tea, and think about her caseload the next day.

Carol

'Why are things any better now?' Moira said.

'What do you mean?'

'I mean, I suppose, what I say.' A pause. 'Many things were worse in the nineteenth century. I'm sure that's right. I'm just interested in why you think it's right.'

Carol looked over the table at her friend. Moira was still staring down at the newspaper but after a moment she lifted her two hands to her temple in a smooth and symmetric movement, carefully detached her reading glasses, and raised her eyes.

Her friend, as Carol sometimes introduced her.

She smiled, though Moira's expression remained still, the mask-like hint of disapproval that of a tutor to a favoured student. Carol almost wanted to kiss her.

'You know why.'

The first hint of a smile. 'Not that.'

And then she did lean forward and kiss her.

Relaxing back into her chair Carol sighed. 'Well, there's the obvious. Medicine, the levelling of the class structure, transport, communication …'

'Aren't these things relative?'

'How so?'

'Well, from the point of view of the Victorians they had themselves made vast strides in all those areas compared to their own predecessors a century before. If I desire to travel from London to Newcastle, and the advent of the steam train facilitates that wish, is that not precisely the same as wishing to travel from London to Sydney courtesy of British Airways?'

'Your point?'

'We desire only what we can imagine. Nowadays we imagine more, so we desire more. But the desire remains across the centuries. Can we therefore be different?'

Carol leaned back. She knew that she had one tremendous advantage over all the rest of the members of the writing group. Research. Heaven knew there was enough of that in trying to recreate the texture and the smell of Disraeli's London. But having someone close to hand who had studied and then lectured on that period throughout her professional life, and who was recognised as a minor authority on the economic role of women in that society, certainly eased the process of underpinning her fiction with sufficient factual detail.

At least she would never receive in the post - assuming she got the damn thing published - a certain type of letter - *Dear Ms Baxendale, I thoroughly enjoyed your book. However I must point out a number of factual errors in your descriptions of the costumes worn by young women in Stepney in the 1880s ...*

'What time are you getting back?' Moira said.

'This evening?'

'You are meeting, aren't you?'

Carol looked across the table. 'Why don't you come along afterwards? We'll be in the pub by nine-fifteen.'

'I have some work to do.'

'You sure?'

But on the issue of research, it seemed to Carol, there was a small problem, and Moira was in fact part of it. It concerned the question of veracity, of historical accuracy. The group had spent an hour arguing over two bottles of wine, last time they met, whether this accuracy should be abandoned in favour of what might be called the *semblance* of accuracy. The modern readership had an awareness not only of cliché but also of its imagined opposite. If it had rejected the Hollywood notion of the cheeky chappie, the cockney Sparrow, it nevertheless accepted, perhaps rather too uncritically, the notion of the dark, Satanic mills housing a proletariat unendingly oppressed by an elite of chinless wonders.

The truth, as Moira frequently argued, was more subtly nuanced. 'And writing, even fiction, means nothing unless it is honest.'

'But fiction is not about facts,' Carol would say. 'It is about perceptions as well.'

'Even if those perceptions are false?'

They argued, often, in terms outsiders, even the members of the group, might find arcane and irrelevant. So what if a tenth of a percent or ten percent of women went to university? The point was that ninety percent did not. And now, preparing to leave - it was Peter's house this time, did she have the address on her - she wondered whether the argument masked a subtler divergence, a forking between fiction and history, something that needed to be examined. Somewhere in there lay questions of purpose and essence, of narrative selectivity and vision. Of the power of fiction to strip away - or embellish. Its ability to focus, critique, and finally redeem. And thus to transcend. She stood outside her front door and knew she desperately wanted to say these things to Moira and then remembered she had not said goodbye. For a moment she felt impelled to turn round, open the door, telephone the group to say she was ill - or better, to tell them to go to hell. And then prepare and cook pasta with her own pesto sauce and, later, curl up to watch with her beloved a few back episodes of *The Wire*.

Stan

'Mate, she said she's sorry.'

Peter looked up from the table. Stan stood, his hip leaning into the bar, arms folded in front of him, his left foot hooked around the right, while a young man next to him flicked drops of red wine from his jacket. Jane fumbled in her bag for tissues. Her glass, now empty, lay on its side on a mat in front of a keg of Guinness.

It occurred to Peter that Stan was a useful bloke to have around. The young man, still muttering and frowning, was not about to take issue with Jane, despite the fact that Stan could have been his father. Especially so, it seemed to Pete, when he compared the youth's diminutive frame with Stan's rather fleshy and suntanned forearms.

'Popeye,' Mary whispered at his side.

'What was that?' Moira said, but Peter, noticing the tattoo, saw what she meant.

'Jane, can I help?' Carol called out. It was rare enough that Jane joined them in the pub after writers' group. And now this.

'All sorted,' Stan said, as he walked over from the bar and placed his pint and a re-filled glass for Jane down on the table. The others shifted in their chairs to make room as they sat down.

Peter had to smile. There was some debate in the group as to how much of what Stan told them was true. None, said Carol. The debate of course occurred only on those occasions when he was not present, or, rather charmingly, after his daughter had come to pick him up and ensure he made it home, an array of empty pint glasses by then scattered around the table. His daughter who, it had turned out, was the somewhat less-than-charming senior partner at a corporate law firm.

The story of his childhood, unremittingly grim, the details of which he insisted on reading out to them whenever opportunity allowed, seemed at times so bleak as to be more a parody of working class life in the slums of a port town as it might have been in the fifties and sixties. The alcoholic mother, the stream of 'gentleman' visitors. The absent father. The beatings. And later on, the knifings and the drugs.

And now he seemed so at ease when faced with the admittedly slighter threat of violence which had just now flickered at the bar. They had seen it before, on a number of ocasions, once when a fist fight erupted two tables away at the very same pub. It was Stan who quickly separated the combatants - *leave it to me, mateys, I know what this is all about* - and then shepherded them outside to resolve their differences in private.

But sometimes the group would just stare open-mouthed when he related an incident from his childhood years. Like the time he discovered what sex was when he found out that the twelve year old next door had been regularly assaulted by her father.

'You can't include that,' Jane had said. 'It's so ... oh, my word ...'

'Why not? It happened.'

'It's just ...'

'Stan -' this from Moira, the one person who, perhaps because she was not part of the group, seemed to have Stan's measure '- you need to be a bit careful. People might be able to trace the girl. Now you don't want that, do you?'

He thought about it for precisely two seconds. 'OK. I'll make her a boy.'

Supper at Walter and Jane's

'You didn't.'
'I did.'
'How could you?'
'It was only one night.'
'But he's …'
'Well, two.'
'…loathsome. I saw him on TV. Bald, slimy, overweight.'
'It was thirty years ago. He was different then.'
'So were we.'
'He was rather gorgeous.'
'God, yes, he was.'
'So what was it like?'

Madeleine smiled at the other women. 'Now that would be telling.'

The three men at the table were silent, perhaps contemplating, with a degree of antipathy, the modern day success of their one time rival.

Richard gazed across at his wife. She was still beaming at Jane and Zoe. It was somehow a tradition of Richard's marriage, never formally spelled out but nevertheless binding, that Madeleine revealed her past conquests - all of them before they were married, of course - whereas he did not. It never failed to irritate him that she did this. She never spotted it, he hid his annoyance well. Or perhaps, it occurred to him now, she did notice but continued to do it nevertheless.

On this occasion the reminiscence was more galling than usual. He had seen the man in question on the late-night news in a report from a Frankfurt trade fair. Bald, slimy and indeed overweight, he had spoken forcefully of the need for national belt-tightening, his jowly and overfed face quivering as he asserted the necessity of a new economic self-discipline. Just weeks before on the same programme Richard had caught a glimpse in a marching crowd of his youngest - Will, supposedly at school that day - as a segment covered the latest round of government retrenchments. He had shouted at the lad as he slunk off to his room - *Will, that's you. Oy. Come back here. That was you* - yet had felt at the same time a wave of almost intoxicating pride.

A pride he did not reveal to Madeleine.

'Is anyone still in contact with him?' said Jane.

Richard snorted.

'What?'

'Nothing,' he said to his wife.

'Who'd have thought it?'

'Thought what?'

'That he'd become so successful.'

'I would,' said Madeleine - *I bet that's true*, Richard thought - 'Wouldn't you?' she added.

Walter cleared his throat. 'He always seemed to me very ... smooth.'

'He certainly knew how to charm,' said Zoe.

'How did you know him, Walt?' said Jane, the only of them all who had not studied - and come of age - at the town's university.

'He sold me his stereo. The day he graduated. Said he was trading up. I got fleeced.'

Richard poured himself another glass of wine, and then, as an afterthought, moved to refill the glasses of everyone else.

Supper at Walter and Jane's

'No thanks,' said Anton. 'But ... you know -' he began to stroke his chin '- I always find it interesting, who's made it, who's not.'

'Seems all rather random to me,' said Madeleine.

Zoe said, 'Are you implying we haven't?'

Anton's thumb and forefinger caressed the skin below his downturned mouth, a gesture which at least two of the women could recollect him doing thirty years before, though against flesh considerably smoother - in the case of one of them, as he lay propped up over her, one knee either side of her naked hips, his own jeans and pants scattered somewhere on the floor around them.

'None of us is wealthy,' he said softly and precisely. 'Well off. Sure. But - I'm guessing - not wealthy. Unless someone here has that proverbial great uncle with a fortune in Argentina.'

'Well off?' said Jane. 'Excuse me, have you never heard of teenage children?'

'So who is?' said Zoe. 'Who's filthy rich? From the old crowd?'

Jules, thought Anton.

'Ed whats-his-name. Martini, I always say. Isn't he some ghastly banker?'

'Santini. Commodity trader. Last I heard Ed was living in Switzerland.'

Jules, thought Richard.

'That weirdo, Anton, the one who did maths with you.'

'Russ?'

'That's it.'

'Russ Sparks. I knew him at school. His father was pretty dodgy.'

'What does he do?'

'Football, I think. Owns a string of clubs up north.'

Jules, thought Zoe.

'How did he make his money?'

'Who? Russ?'

'He wasn't really the college type, was he?'
'Not middle class enough?'
'Bad teeth.'
'Anton?'
'Scrap metal or something,' he said. 'That's where he made his dosh.'
'Jules,' said Walter. 'Jules, of course.'
There was silence.

Jules. Of course. Julia, the serial entrepreneur. From coffee-shops in the eighties, to dot-com froth in the nineties, to furnishing and fine style for Chinese billionaires more recently. Now ennobled, for services to industry, as Anton had recently read in the Times.

In a way he was surprised that her name had arisen, and yet if it was to come up it was perhaps inevitable that Walter had mentioned it. He wondered how much Jane knew, or guessed.

Anton remembered the first few years in London after they graduated. Walter had followed Julia up to town, unable to accept that the carnal and fiery relationship they shared in their final student year had burnt itself out by the time they received their degrees. At least in Julia's eyes. She was leaving childhood behind, she was already moving on, networking within a smarter crowd, seeking out, sometimes seducing, every bowtied mover and double-breasted shaker she could find. Walter trailed in her wake, tolerated but never indulged. Whenever Anton met him he seemed to be living a strange kind of binary existence, whose twin states were those of elation when a re-ignition of the passion seemed possible, of despair when it came to nothing. Walter had never been a drinker at university, but, those years of his early twenties, he was always smashed or hungover.

Jane had rescued him from this, perhaps without realising it, when she persuaded him to leave London and settle back in the provinces.

'Julia, of course,' said Walter. His eyes were lowered. 'But I guess that was no surprise to anyone.'

Supper at Walter and Jane's

Anton observed him. He felt an impulse, which he had to resist, to reach a hand across and touch the sleeve of his shirt.

He knew that Walter's bitterness would never entirely evaporate.

The six people around the table met every two or three years, and as they passed into their fifties the changes one noticed between successive meetings became ever fewer.

*

Jane sat at her dressing table rubbing cream into her face.

'Well that went well.' She addressed her words to Walter's reflection in the mirror.

'Hmm.' He was lying in bed with an unopened plastic bound folder in front of him. He opened his eyes only for a moment as the slam of the front door sent a tremor through the house.

'That's Sean,' said Jane. She was still for a second, straining to hear teenage voices.

Jane wondered whether her son was drunk. She had been rather shocked recently when Walter announced with some glee that Sean had bought him a beer at a local pub. *But he's under-age*, she had said. *Come on*, he said, *we were the same*. He added, *At least I was*.

'Did you hear from Mary?' she said.

'Hmm.'

'Walt?'

The folder, work he had brought home, slipped off the bed. 'Staying at …' - a grunted profanity - '… at Toni's, I think.'

'Language. Walter.' Jane was momentarily put out that the oath should occur in the same breath as the name of their daughter's closest friend.

She listened once more. There was silence downstairs. Sean had evidently not brought any fellow inebriates home with him.

'That went well,' she said again. 'Do you think Anton will be OK in the annex?'

'He'll be fine.' This mumbled.

'You know ...' Jane put the top onto the pot of cold cream and turned to her husband. '... You know, I always feel that Anton and Zoe make a nice couple. Don't you think?'

Walter was pretending to sleep.

'Come on, he's your best friend. What do you think?' She got up, walked over and picked the folder up off the floor, then moved to the other side of the bed and climbed in. 'Walter?' There was no answer. She lay propped up, her head against the bed rest. 'Well, at least there'll be no shenanigans between those two,' she said, her eyes closing. It had been decided that Zoe would stay with Richard and Madeleine, and Anton with them. 'Not tonight.'

Jane reached across to switch off the light, and then paused. She decided to leave it on for a few moments, in the hope that she might prod Walter into talking. But his breathing had steadied and deepened in the way she knew so well. *And no shenanigans here either.*

She thought of Anton - he still looked good, his thin and angular features and ascetically short grey hair giving him something of the look of a priest. Men were luckier than women. For them - *for us*, she thought - looks were so tied to youth. Some of her girlfriends were racked by what they perceived as the cosmic injustice of this. Especially when their ex-husbands found themselves young - and mortifyingly inappropriate - new partners. But for Jane, permanently overweight, resigned to the ripples under her chin, it had never been an issue, perhaps because she saw herself living more and more - in a strange way almost reborn - through her daughter, these days so lissome and delightful.

She had often asked Walter why Anton had never married - he had never in the years she had known him even had a regular relationship. Walter's explanations seemed always rather too

Supper at Walter and Jane's

metaphysical, as if Anton were indeed following some higher path. 'But doesn't he ... miss it?' she would think of saying, and then would not, as if to do so might stretch Walter's intimacy with his friend too far.

Is he gay? she would ask herself, but would turn away from this line of enquiry when its consequence - that her own husband might once himself have explored similar leanings, perhaps with Anton - forced itself into her mind. *Would he ever tell me if he had?* she thought now, turning to look at the sleeping form of her husband. *Would you ever say, my dear?*

Jane turned on to her other side, reached and switched off the light. She pulled the duvet up to her chin and imagined the naked body of Anton pressed against her back, bony arms and legs reaching around her. And yet the image remained peculiarly sexless. She remembered now - it came to her as something of a shock that she could forget this - the warmth of her husband's erection nestling between her legs. And, as sleep hovered, the rigid flesh of other lovers from earlier years.

*

'More salad, anyone?'

'Here, let me help you with the dishes.'

'Jane, the salmon was wonderful.'

'Thank Walter. He did most of the hard work this afternoon.'

'Here's to Jane and Walter, then,' said Zoe. 'Oops. Any more white wine?'

There was a gathering of plates and cutlery. Madeleine and Jane were on their feet.

'Who's watching the football tomorrow?'

Walter rose and walked into the kitchen. 'What time?' His shouted voice carried from the other room.

'It's on Sky,' Richard said. 'I always said' - his voice boomed - 'I would refuse on principle to add a penny to the Murdoch coffers. But …'

Walter reappeared with a bottle in his hand.

A whisper. '… I've succumbed.'

'What's all this football?' said Zoe. 'Bit Nick Hornby, isn't it? Since when were you lot so sporty?'

'Not me,' said Anton.

'I can't remember any of you ever raising a sweat when we were students.'

'That's unfair, Zoe,' said Richard. 'I used to play tennis. I was good.'

'I never knew that,' said Anton. 'You never invited me to a game.'

Richard did not reply.

'We played a few times,' Walter said as he uncorked the bottle. 'Rich? Didn't we? You always won, if I remember.'

Richard still said nothing.

'Do any of your children play?' said Zoe.

Richard sighed. 'Will, a bit. School makes him. Anthea, Luke. Nah, never.'

'Do I detect a note of parental disappointment?' said Zoe.

'We never pushed them,' said Madeleine. 'Did we, Richard?'

'What about you, Walter?' said Zoe.

Walter poured Zoe a glass of white wine, slowly, and with a twist of the neck of the bottle as the glass filled. 'No.' The single word seemed to snuff out the discussion, and Walter had no intention of resuscitating it. He had no desire to revisit the trouble he had taken to ensure that his own children never had to endure the winter afternoons of cross-country or the endless after-school rugby that his own father had inflicted upon him.

'We're not really very sporty, are we?' said Zoe. 'The six of us?'

'I go to the gym,' said Madeleine. 'We do try, don't we, Richard?'

Supper at Walter and Jane's

'I like my yoga,' said Jane returning to the living room for more plates.

'I suppose,' said Zoe with a snigger, 'we're just a bit weedy.'

Walter remained standing. He caressed the stem of his wine glass between his thumb and forefinger. *They're all a bit weedy, your friends,* his father had said the first time his parents visited him at his college hall. *Don't you know any marathon runners? Do this lot even know how to play footie?* His father, whom he had wept over and eulogised at the club fifty yards from the family home - barely a hundred from the churchyard where he had buried him two hours before - that same harriers club where his father had been in turn four minute miler, captain, treasurer, secretary, and finally saloon bar bore when a younger generation picked up the courage to move him aside.

'I wonder,' said Jane. 'Did we make a mistake? There's so much money in it these days.'

'I know,' said Madeleine. 'I sometimes feel guilty that we never encouraged the kids a bit more. Even if it's only management. Or … what do they call it …'

'Agenting,' said Richard. 'That's the term, dear. In all its grammatical inelegance.'

'God knows, there's so little else out there for them now. I do worry so.'

Anton cleared his throat. 'How old are they? Your children?'

'Luke's graduated,' said Madeleine. 'Twenty-three. Anthea's still at Leeds …'

'What do they want to do?'

'What can they do?' said Richard. 'With this bloody government.'

'What do they want to do?' Anton repeated. 'Madeleine?'

'Luke's got something part-time. Some internet startup in Hoxton. Anthea, well, she's still not sure.'

'None of them fancy the City?' said Anton.

'God, please, spare us,' said Richard.

'Richard,' said Madeleine.

'Well if this government will insist on robbing the poor …'

'Come on, Richard,' said Anton. 'That's a bit …'

'… to pay a bunch of obscenely rewarded bankers …'

'You can hardly blame this government when the last lot did so much to bankrupt the country.'

'Yes I can. Why aren't they doing something positive? For young people?'

'Like what?'

'Like supporting the businesses of the future.'

'Like what?'

'Like manufacturing.'

'With respect, Richard, … '

'Since when did we forget how to make things?'

'… with respect, since when did you actually buy something British?'

'The only reason we bloody well can't …' Richard's voice was rising '… was that bloody woman.'

'Woman?'

Walter watched his friends arguing. *Manufacturing, my boy. Why aren't you doing engineering?* His father had never forgiven him for choosing to study English Literature. *Or physics?* And now he was having to ask himself, was his father right? Had he and his contemporaries betrayed a generation by eschewing the kinds of courses, and then the professions, where you worked outside the office and where you actually created something which had three dimensions, with mass and substance, which you could sell to the Japanese? By treating such courses with contempt? And now, wasn't there something ludicrous about this conversation between the friends he first met when those choices were irrevocably made?

'You know who I mean. She destroyed it all. In the eighties.'

'That's rather a mischaracterisation. If I may say so.'

Zoe was laughing. 'Come on chaps.' Perhaps a sense of the same absurdity had passed through her mind. 'I really can't see any of you lot with a hard hat or a lab coat or slide rule.'

Supper at Walter and Jane's

'Slide rule?'

'Or even a screwdriver.'

She was right, thought Walter. Absolutely right. What could they, the six of them, the gilded generation who had robbed their children and grandchildren to pay for their career satisfaction and their pretensions and their Dordogne cottages, what could they say about the decline of Britain's economy? Law, HR (was that what Jane called it?), the BBC, Madeleine's children's clotheshop. And he himself, director of strategy ('downsizer-in-chief', as Sean mischievously put) of a quango whose function he could no longer explain without recourse to a jargon as opaque as the Anglo-Saxon he had once studied.

The thought of them as champions of British industry was, he knew, quite risible.

'Anyway, look at Jules,' said Anton.

'What, selling *lifestyle* to filthy rich Arabs?'

'She's out there. She's creating businesses.'

'That … froth?'

'It's called free enterprise, Richard. That's the future.'

Richard was on his feet. 'Excuse me,' he muttered. He headed for the loo. *Fuck it*, they heard as he tripped on the stairs.

*

The taxi doors slammed shut. Richard waited until it had driven one hundred yards before he snorted.

'Richard,' said Zoe.

'Aaargh. That Anton. I can't stand it.'

'What?'

'I can't stand *him*.'

'But he's one of your best pals.'

'No he's not'

'You were so close at uni.'

'Walt's friend. Not mine.'

'Richard, you can't mean that.'
'And his politics. He's such a fascist.'

Sitting in the front next to the driver, the man bearded, silent except sometimes to mumble what sounded like a prayer - she noticed the beads entwined around the rearview mirror - Madeleine let Richard's rant pass over her as she always did. She hoped it would have exhausted itself by the time they got home. For now she needed a few moments to gather her thoughts together.

She had been unnerved by the frequent references to Julia.

When he emailed a month before to say he was setting up the reunion, Walter had indicated he would try to get her to come down from London and join them. Madeleine had immediately begun to consider excuses. A pre-planned visit to her sick mother, an invented sales conference in Manchester. Perhaps an attack of the flu.

For the truth was that thirty years before she had fought a long guerrilla campaign against her, a dirty war whose prize was Richard's affection. A war of which the others, even Richard himself, had only cursory knowledge. A war which she had won.

Julia had been his girlfriend for the entirety of their second undergraduate year. Yet she, Madeleine, had been the one who walked away with the prize, a prize which defined every part of her adult life. Her home was the one she shared with Richard. Her children were the ones he had fathered.

And Julia never had the courtesy to recognise this victory. Instead she flounced off to London, found a string of new partners, of whom poor Walter had been one, she knew, and from there planned a different path to the summits. Julia had cut her dead at her moment of triumph, and Madeleine would not forgive her.

In bad moments she wondered whether Richard ever regretted his choice. Even more so when the conversation turned to Julia's recent successes as it did this evening. It pained

Supper at Walter and Jane's

her that his stated disdain for her ambition and materialism might instead mask an admiration, even a desire to imagine a *what-if*, the other life that he might have lived.

Madeleine shivered. She pulled her coat tight around her.

Richard and Zoe in the back were still anatomising the evening.

She remembered her gaffe, her indiscretion concerning her one-time lover - *bald, slimy and overweight*, his name for the moment escaped her. Why had she mentioned that appalling man? She knew it irritated Richard.

But the answer was obvious. *Look at me*, she was saying. *I gave up all that. For you.*

She pulled down the passenger side visor. There was a mirror attached. She checked her face, her eyes, her lips. Then she looked at the reflection of the man seated in the back - his hair still full and not yet grey, his long legs hunched up behind the driver's seat.

He was still lecturing Zoe about fascism.

For you.

*

'Coffee anyone?'

'Say, shall we decamp to the sofa?'

'Anyone for more dessert? …'

Richard and Madeleine remained at the table but got up as Walter picked up his glass and led the way. 'Anyone for a *digestif?*,' he said, trumping his wife. 'I might have a bottle hidden away somewhere.'

'… it'll just go to the cat …'

Anton watched Richard go. There was something about the exchange they had just had, an acerbity beyond the give and take one might expect at the dinner table. An intuition about Richard's perception of him hovered at the rim of consciousness.

'Anton, talk to me.' Zoe still sat opposite him. Her hands were laid on the table, a gesture of decisiveness, as if she were about to press herself up. 'Tell me about yourself.'

He looked into her wide eyes, those youthful brown eyes in her now lined face.

'Same old job,' he said. 'American multinational. Pharmaceuticals.'

'So you do make things. Sort of.'

'Not me. I head up the stats division.'

'Stats?'

'Well, we need to know whether our super-expensive drugs might actually kill someone.'

'And do they?'

Anton smiled. *Good old Zoe*, he thought. 'Trade secret.' *Good old sceptical Zoe*. 'What about you?'

Anton thought of Zoe and Jules at university. The closest of friends, Jules had maintained a rather protective manner to Zoe in the years since, as if to provide some kind of shield to the childlike quality she still possessed. The story went that Jules had stood guarantee for the mortgage on her flat.

'Oh, a bit of this, a bit of that,' she said.

'Still producing? Still at the BBC?'

'Less so these days, I'm afraid. Cuts, you know.'

'What else then?'

'The Centre. That keeps me pretty occupied.'

Anton knew that she worked at a hostel for refugees on the outskirts of the seaside town where she lived.

'I'm always getting midnight calls from social services. Some Ghanaian chap with no papers. Albanian kid in trouble after a fight.'

'It's very good of you,' said Anton. 'You know …' He paused, wondering whether what he was about to say sounded pretentious. '… you're the only one of us who's got a tiny bit of … of what I'd call … just plain goodness.'

'Don't be silly.'

Supper at Walter and Jane's

Anton was pierced by an access of sadness. He had overheard a conversation between the three women in the kitchen before they all sat down to eat. *Well, at least there are some advantages.* It had been Zoe's voice. *No more shaving under the armpits. No more waxing.* He knew they had been talking about growing old.

'I mean it,' he said.

He stared at her. That pixie-like charm which she had had as an eighteen year old. It was still there.

'I mean it,' he repeated softly.

Walter was hovering over them with six fresh glasses in his hands. 'Come on, you two. Join the rest of us.'

Anton waited for Zoe to rise, and followed her and Walter over to the other side of the room. The others sat on cushions on the floor or on the settees. He remained standing for a second, then walked back to the dinner table, picked up a hard-backed chair and carried it over.

'Anton, over here.' Jane patted the place next to her.

'I'm fine,' said Anton. 'Honestly.'

'Right,' said Walter. 'Who's for a drop? Twelve years old.'

Anton looked at Walter pouring, and then at the other four faces watching him. For some reason he thought again of Jules. Once, a long time ago, it had been perhaps five years after they had left university, he met her by chance at a party in London. They ended up in bed together. The two of them lay entwined in each other's arms, talking till dawn and beyond on a luminous Sunday morning in the Battersea flat she then owned. They slept a few hours, and had coffee and croissants at an Italian café nearby. She told him she was leaving for Hong Kong the very next week and they would not be seeing each other for a while.

But make me a promise, she said.
What's that?
Marry me.
Now?
When we're forty. When we're old.

He had laughed. But as he left her to walk to the tube, crumpled in the previous day's clothes, he turned and called out, *OK, it's a deal.* And twenty yards on, louder, *Just - just don't ever forget.*

It would be two decades before he saw her again, when she contacted him out of the blue for advice on her second son's maths papers.

'Anton. Here.' Walter handed him a glass. 'Is that everyone? Zoe?'

'Not for me, thanks. Wine is fine.'

'Oh well. Chin chin.'

He never did tell any of this to Walter. And nor would he.

'A toast.'

'To whom?'

'To …'

… *absent lovers*, thought Anton.

*

Zoe pulled the duvet around her and closed her eyes.

It was so quiet here. Unlike her third floor flat off the seafront. No police sirens. No drunken screams. So quiet.

She felt exhausted. She had so enjoyed the evening, it was wonderful to see them all again. But now she was tired. Now she wanted to be alone.

She thought about what she had lined up for the coming week. There wasn't really very much. Zoe had dissembled somewhat about her work at the BBC. It wasn't that it had tailed off. The truth was, it had stopped, and it had stopped years before. Her days, apart from the Centre, were pretty much empty.

On Tuesday she would accompany Hanif and Kareem to the passport office to get their visas renewed. That was after the doctors of course. On Wednesday - she absolutely mustn't

Supper at Walter and Jane's

forget - she would call her mother at the nursing home in Aberdeen. She hoped her mother was making an effort with the Filipino nurses, there had been such a fuss the month before.

Next weekend, there was, well … laundry, library, Sainsburys. Later, a bottle of Chardonnay and Kate Winslet on TV.

That was next week.
But now …
She stretched. Everything here was just so quiet.
So quiet …
So …

She turned over, pulled her knees up close, and massaged the skin beneath her left breast.

Walter was sweet. In the darkness Zoe smiled. They all were. Of course. But Walter especially. Just as he had been at eighteen.

She had wondered earlier whether to tell them, to tell *him*, about her condition. About her latest visits to the hospital. Good thing she hadn't. It would have been just too much. Anyway, they would find out soon enough.

She must be more careful. Must cut down on the booze, she'd had much too much this evening. *In vino veritas*. All that had to stop. She must listen to what the consultants were telling her …

Oh, Walter. That boy from the provinces. Sunlight on his face. Those NHS specs, those flared jeans.

It's so quiet here, she thought once more.
Zoe began to tremble.
So quiet.
So …

*

'Richard, that's our taxi.'

'I didn't hear anything.'

'Listen.' They were silent. After five seconds there was a clipped beep from a car horn.

Richard fumbled with his mobile. 'Yep. I've got a text.'

Everyone was standing.

'Walter. Jane. What a wonderful evening.'

'Fantastic food.'

'We must do it again.'

'Soon.'

'Our place next time.'

'Come to Hastings. All of you. Anton, you as well.'

'Here, I'll get your coats'.

The women embraced and kissed. The men shook hands. Jane moved to the window, drew aside the curtain and waved to the driver. Walter walked in from the hallway, three coats on his arm.

Richard and Madeleine and Zoe passed a jumble of wool between them. Gloves. Hats. Scarves. There was another round of hugs and handshakes. Walter stood at the front door.

Jane shrieked. 'Wait.'

Everyone paused.

'Wait. All of you.' Walter frowned. 'Just a second,' she said.

She rushed up the stairs. They heard one door slam, another open. Once she called out, *Walt, don't let them go*.

She rushed down. She carried a large photograph in a silver frame.

'Look. Here.'

They all crowded round. It was a picture of a dozen teenagers. The boys looked gawky and unsure in black tie and dinner jacket. The women, mature and more confident, were dressed in evening gowns.

'What's this then?'

'That's Sean,' said Jane, pointing. 'Isn't he handsome?'

Supper at Walter and Jane's

'School prom?'

'We never had those.'

'And there's Mary. Sean managed to smuggle her an invite.'

The six friends pressed closer together and stared. In the shadowy light of the hallway, the outline of their reflections flickered back at them off the glass of the picture frame. For the first time all evening they were silent.

A car horn sounded.

The Room

He placed a hand against the fashioned brass of the door handle, twisted, and pressed lightly. The door swung open, its movement even and ponderous. Darkness inside. He shone his torch left and right, up and down. Tall ceilings, the beam of light fading in the far corners. Curtains hung thick from the opposite wall, drawn close as if to deaden all sound and frivolous activity from the outside world. To the left, a massive desk, extending most of the width of the room. To the right, a cabinet of shelves, rows and rows of books, hardback, meticulously arranged in order of size, sloping tallest to shortest.

He padded over to the cabinet and ran the torchlight against the stained brown of the wood. And then, stretching, traced a finger along the smoothed mahogany bearing the uppermost line of books. Motes of dust caught in the narrow beam. Yet the shelves at shoulder level below were wiped and polished, as if the furniture had enjoyed the merely perfunctory attentions of the cleaner - maid or home help, perhaps - someone who felt little affection for the antique craftsmanship. One set of books stood apart, matte black, gold lettering on the spine, all the same shape and thickness, as in a collection. The lives of the great scientists. He moved the torch along. Eddington, Edison, Einstein, Faraday. It looked as if they had not been taken down in an age, and he wondered whether they were there for show only, but, thinking again, he knew that that was absurd, that perhaps instead his man simply knew everything there was that the books had to say.

He moved across to the other side of the room. A single straight backed chair stood behind the desk. He sat. A PC lay to the right, the one concession to modernity in this room, it seemed, and yet even here, with its ultra slim-line monitor, matte black, pushed to the far corner of the desk surface, its footprint seemed almost erased from the living space. Before him, two sheets of paper, laid neatly and in parallel beside a table lamp. He bent close. Arrays of symbols. Unintelligible, the complexity of the universe reduced to a concise abstraction. Then he realised something. Not a single picture in the room. He looked around. No. He saw one, just one. The old man on a podium, uneasy in tails, some certificate in his hands, flunkeys applauding at his side.

He felt down to his left. Drawers. Locked. He drew out the keys he had been given, and opened them one by one. Blank paper, stationery, old documents. He searched further. In the bottom drawer, under a stack of decades old issues of *Scientific American*, a photograph, black and white, its edges yellowed. His man, with a full head of dark hair, next to another man and a woman, a couple perhaps. All of them smiling. A sly ambivalence in the set of her eyes. He turned the picture over. *Anna and Gerhard. 1967.* And for the first time he felt he was genuinely intruding. He paused, but for just a second, and reached in again. More correspondence, with the University, with colleagues abroad. And then, slipping from between them like blossom shaken from a tree, a single sheet of letter paper, the longhand faded, a quality of lost elegance and subtle self-disclosure in the fineness of the calligraphy.

He read. *My dearest, dearest Anna, ...*

Freeway

Andy, Rick and Dee stood in the queue at the immigration desk. A grey man in a blue uniform and steel-capped boots sat in a raised glass booth checking entries in a massive black ledger. Rick, fooling around, joked that the old tosser looked like his old Beowulf tutor. Guards with pistols stood silent and dark. Other flight passengers frowned at his levity.

The next day they climbed the Empire State, they ate falafel at a Lebanese takeaway in Greenwich Village, they saw streets which, hemmed in by eighty storey buildings, seemed somehow more spacious, more vibrant and filled with possibility, with humanity, than any others they had walked down. They bussed to Washington D.C., rucksacks stuffed in racks above their heads. They had contacts, one or two numbers, but they ignored them and found jobs in bars and clubs. They moved in with students. They worked all hours of the day, harder than they ever could have imagined. They bought pot at a party from a respectable black lady and panicked when she let slip as calm as you like that she was FBI.

Nights, they sat like hicks out on the porch in the humid air. They smoked joints and pipes and stared, stoned, at the sky. Then, late one evening as they finished work, new found friends drove them to Atlantic City. They arrived as the sun rose. They ate crab and shellfish at an all-you-can-eat, one plate after another, and then slept, bloated, on the beach.

They travelled.

They delivered cars, old wrecks, but newer models as well, limousines with leather seats and air-conditioning. They cut through Virginia and the Carolinas, they switched cars at a faded beach front outside Miami and drove as far south as the roads would take them onto the Keys. Beneath a perfect sky, they rested and sunbathed, they sat amongst the gay crowd and the slackers, scanning the horizon for the Castro menace. Soon, another job, another delivery, and they were pounding out five hundred miles a day. Cities and states came and went, Tampa, Pensacola, New Orleans, Baton Rouge. They crossed flood plains and vast river deltas, they travelled on bridges, arched or suspended constructions of steel and concrete, their span seeming to stretch from one horizon to another They got stopped by the cops, and escaped jail when they swore on their lives they would be out of the state the following day. They skirted round the north of Texas, they saw deserts and dust plains. They bought coke and burritos at roadside stops where they were invited to discover Jesus. Insects, prehistoric in size and shape and colour, milled and danced in a frenzy around the suspended spot lights, and then, instincts and radar frazzled and burnt, came crashing into people, into their soup bowls, windscreens, anything that stood in their way.

They stopped at Dallas and Fort Worth. At a diner, they parked and sat gawping as a tarantula lowered itself from the overhanging roof onto the bonnet of a truck. They headed north into Colorado and the mountains, the temperature plummeted in a day, and people stared and pointed when they got out of their cars in shorts and t-shirts.

Impelled westward, fuelled by packs of Marlboro and Winston, they left Denver, crossed the mountains and dropped thousands of feet into the unnerving calm of Salt Lake City, its tranquillity and order bizarre, so at odds with the frantic vision of the men and women who, a century before, had trail blazed the same path. They crossed deserts, they stumbled and cursed when they burnt their feet stepping onto the road out of the refrigerated microclimate of the Cadillac they drove. And then they sensed a change in the air, an accumulation of signals and pointers around them, from the language of the road signs, informal, almost conversational, to the mirror shades and vanity of the traffic police. They had crossed into California. At a beach just north of San Francisco, the road ended, they got out the car and walked barefoot onto the sand. They did cartwheels, dropped to their knees and stared out over the blue of the Pacific.

They split up and hitched down to Los Angeles. They picked a hotel from the guide and arranged to meet the next day. Andy wondered whether he would see the others again. The weather grew tropical, he saw palm trees beneath skyscrapers, business men with briefcases and Hawaiian shirts. He arrived late at the rendezvous, where an old timer, down-and-out, sitting in the lobby, told him he would find his two buddies at a nearby bar. The next day they met a mouse, a dog and a duck. They rode space mountain. They dressed up Rocky Horror style for a visit to the city's Chinese cathedral of film. On a hill overlooking Hollywood, taking pictures as the sky darkened, they argued over the cost of a hot dog and, months of adrenaline and euphoria going pop in an instant, had a huge row. Time had run out. They began to think of jobs and careers back home. Two days later Dee confirmed her flight out and they prepared to look forward to an English reality stretching away, wet and cold. They left separately, Andy's flight the last to go. The luxury of youth was gone, time would become a precious resource, in future to be rationed and rigorously metered.

This freedom they would know again only in memory.

The Escape

Part One

I

She glanced at her blurred reflection in the frosted glass of the door as she walked up to the office. She fumbled with her keys and frowned. A sense of distraction, a feeling that mind and body were out of phase, had remained with her since she got up that morning, and she felt it once more as she tried to extract the right key for the lock. She opened the door, walked briskly over to the alarm system keypad, and entered the passcode. She saw, but only half registered, the flashing lights on the console, the image fading from memory as she turned towards the meeting room and immediately stumbled over something on the floor. A soft curse. She recovered her footing, looked back, and saw a couple of books thrown loosely over the doorway. She paused, wondering how she could possibly have left them out when she locked up last Friday. And then, slowly, clues cascading into her awareness in an accelerating stream, she began to look round the room and to understand that a hostile presence had invaded this space. A box of computer paper lay scattered chaotically at one corner, the phone line ended, bare, on the conference table, drawers were open, contents, torn, broken and scattered. The overhead projector - where? Gone.

She took her phone from her bag, started to call the police, and then stopped. *Get out. Leave. Leave now. Phone from outside.* But she couldn't. She began to walk round the rest of the office. The kitchen was a mess, there were broken coffee cups on the table, a half empty bottle of whisky beside them. Her reception area was worse. She felt a prick of tears. Her personal belongings, her photos, on the floor. Her switchboard gone. She stared. What else? Fax, calculator. She moved into the main open-plan work area. No PCs. Not one, all gone, sockets wrenched from the wall, pens, paper, books, disks littered over the carpet. A grey stain marked the wall. Someone had thrown a viscous liquid against it from chest height and it had dripped to the floor. She approached, sniffed, and retreated. And then almost vomited.

She moved on to Stewart's room. The door was three quarters closed, and, pushing it open, she saw that the blinds were down, blocking off all light except where they had been forcibly pulled apart. She surveyed the room, and saw the same mess, books and papers all over the floor, computer sockets yanked loose, a desk on its side, the chair facing at an angle towards the window, one of its castors missing. She moved towards it, then stopped, suddenly gasping for breath as she saw the outline of a figure slumped in the chair. She remained still for a couple of seconds, frozen, a tension churning in her stomach. Then, a voice.

'It's OK, I've already called the police. They should be here in a couple of minutes.'

She started to breathe again, her heart beginning to slow. She approached the chair, started to speak, stopped. Stewart did not move. She turned to the blinds, struggled with the cords and managed to open them. She took a deep breath, walked over to another chair, and collapsed into it. She let out a long sigh and looked at Stewart. He was unmoving, staring at a point on the wall where a painting had been dislodged and lay at an angle, its glass front broken. He hadn't moved since she entered the room.

'So when did this all happen?' she finally asked.

The Escape

'God knows. Weekend. At night. I don't know. Could have been anytime.'

She sighed again, placed her bag on the floor, and waited a few seconds.

'You OK, Stewart? Is there anything you need?'

He remained still for a few seconds, then raised a hand and passed his fingers through his hair. He breathed in deeply. After a minute he began to stir in his chair.

'I'm fine. It's just … just an office. No one's hurt. Let's .. '. He scratched his head again.

He got up.

'I'll make some coffee. We better start tidying up.'

Dawn got up and moved into the hall. The buzzer rang. She opened the door. Two policemen stood there, hats in hands, one with a briefcase.

'Stewart Brunswick?'

'Yes. Please. Come in.'

Over their shoulder, she could see a couple of the others now, a hundred yards away, and waited for them to approach.

'Hang on a second' she said to the police officers. She shouted. 'Bob, Mike,' and, more softly, to the police, 'My colleagues.'

She watched them walk towards her, a cloak of Monday morning grey over them. They had noticed the police car. Their pace quickened as they walked up to the door. They looked past her at the officers inside.

'What's going on? What happened?'

'We've had a break-in. Must have been the weekend. The police are here. The place is a mess.'

The two of them hurried in, then stopped.

'God … My PC.'

One of the policemen walked over, asking them to leave everything untouched until they had completed their initial inspection. Bob and Mike stood listlessly in the middle of the room. Dawn handed them cups of coffee. Alicia , their other translator, arrived. The pace began to quicken. The policemen scurried around, a photographer arrived, then a technician for fingerprints. Officers interviewed staff. Stewart, finally roused, began to re-organise his diary for the day.

'Mike, we had the bank people coming this morning. Call them, re-schedule at their place. No, No. Say you'll be there on your own, take notes, and arrange a full meeting later on in the week, try Wednesday.'

'Dawn, do we know what we've lost? Can we get an inventory? Look guys, the most important thing is the data. What have we lost that's critical? Bob, get that IT nerd on the phone, when did we last do a back-up? We need to rent a couple of PCs. Can you get going on that? Thanks.'

The day began to take some shape. Police officers came and went, interviews were completed. Alicia and Mike began to work through the files they could salvage. IT people showed up, machines were installed and connected. Stewart looked at the activity and his depression began to lift.

They're a good crew, he thought, and a light calmness settled on him, a peace that he had not experienced for days, for weeks, at work or at home. He paused, vaguely shocked that this mild elation he felt seemed so rare a feeling, but this lasted just a few seconds as the immediacy of current circumstances forced his attention. He spoke with a detective about motives, he discussed security. He spent half an hour with Alicia, Mike and the IT consultant talking about files, recovering data, back up strategies, and then, bewildered by the foreign language he seemed to speak, left them to talk instead with a carpenter and two glaziers who had just arrived. Next was a call to the bank, then his insurer. Clients followed. Dawn worked on his diary. Mike returned, they sat on the floor, laid out papers around them, and figured out a strategy for the week. They ordered pizzas, ate a quick lunch, and continued the salvage operation. At four o'clock a cheer went up around the office when the data backup was finally complete. The new PCs were switched on, and Dawn shouted out that they were open for business. Stewart retired to his room, shut the door, and began to look at his personal papers.

He had arrived early that Monday morning to spend some time reading journals, mail that had arrived from abroad, his e-mails. The shock from seeing the break-in had hit him like a physical blow, and the fifteen minutes before Dawn had arrived he had sat dazed, unable, unwilling, to take any action. He had worried that some of his personal correspondence may have disappeared, but he was satisfied now that everything was still there, though it had taken a while for it all to be located. He was especially relieved that a parcel from his German relatives had not been taken. He had not yet had a chance to do more than skim through the contents, but it was these, and the cryptic, deliberately mysterious - or so it seemed to him - tone of the covering letter that had left him curious. He had considered phoning his cousin Marta in Munich, she was perhaps the only one of that side of the family he still got on with at all well, but something held him back, perhaps a feeling that with the parcel came some family tension, some rift between them and himself. He picked up the letter and began to read it again. It was from a cousin, Gerhard, what was he? Grandson of his grandmother's oldest sister.

Stewart remembered a fastidious, precise man, a civil servant, early forties, whose courtesy sometimes appeared to conceal an impatience with others. He recalled their last phone conversation a few years ago, re-unification at that time a decade past, with Gerhard about to move, alongside tens of thousands of colleagues, from Bonn to Berlin. Stewart assumed that Gerhard saw himself as head of the family these days, and the contents of the letter seemed to confirm this. Some of it was familiar to Stewart. His great uncle had died two years earlier after a long illness. Werner had lived in a care home for the last ten years of his life, without immediate family to support him.

But the letter then went on in its formal prose to describe how difficult it had been to deal with the estate. Werner's business affairs had been more complex than first thought, there were heirlooms and assets to dispose of. And then there was some difference of opinion in the family as to how and to whom ownership of these assets should be transferred. From the careful wording of the letter, Stewart guessed that disagreement ran deep.

Stewart let his mind wander back to childhood holidays in Germany. He would meet his great uncle frequently, often staying with him in his house outside Munich. The old man lived alone. Stewart found out years later that he had married after the war, but it had not lasted.

For a child, this meant that he could treat this particular adult almost as an older brother. Stewart loved the house, too large for one person, with rooms, drawers, closets that a child could explore and discover. Occasionally he would come across old knick knacks from the war. A soldier's helmet, pictures of men in uniform, a spent cartridge shell. He understood only years later that these toys were Nazi memorabilia.

But this close relationship with his uncle faded as he grew into his late teens. Stewart studied Modern Languages at university, and, influenced by tutors and new friends, had developed a strong sense of a new kind of Europe. His grandparents' generation became an embarrassment, a reminder of times everyone wished to move on from.

His great uncle's education, Stewart knew, had been interrupted by the war, and he had never returned to it. Instead he had worked as a carpenter, a handyman, working from nothing to carve out a life in the great reconstruction that had taken place in Germany in the fifties. He had been moderately successful, building up a business employing twenty or thirty people. But for Stewart, visiting him during one of his summer holidays while at University, his great uncle's life seemed to represent all that Stewart disliked about his country. Stewart spent a day with Werner at his office. He despised Werner's manner with his men - labourers, Turks, refugees from Eastern Europe - at all times curt and overbearing, his day one long fight with grasping suppliers, price obsessed clients and an untrustworthy workforce.

Stewart saw himself instead as part of a new economy, not class-based, driven by visionaries of a borderless European union. His visits dropped off. His great uncle retired at the age of seventy, had a stroke soon after, and had moved into a home for the elderly. Stewart's occasional visits over the next few years had always been unnerving. He found him taciturn, and yet, his memory of events from the far past stronger than of recent years, would be drawn out whenever Stewart inadvertently raised some issue or event from those years. The Great Depression, hyperinflation, the communist threat. And then it irritated him when the nurses told him that his great uncle loved his visits, and that he would talk endlessly and with pride of his British nephew. Stewart remembered his last visit, his great uncle in bed all day. No words were spoken but his simple presence seemed to infuse the old man with a lightness and grace.

He hated himself for his behaviour towards the family at Werner's death. He had not been to the funeral, he had not answered letters or returned phone calls, and even on his business trips to Germany he did not take time to meet them. And it came to him now that the letter from his relatives added to this sense of guilt.

He assumed that his great uncle's era was over. History. Of no concern to him.

Yet the old man had made provision in his will that certain personal papers and artefacts were to be passed on to Stewart.

Specifically Stewart. Owing to the difficulty in finding and then sorting through these papers, it was only now, two years after his death, that Gerhard could execute this particular statement in his will. These items, now collected together, were enclosed in the accompanying parcel. 'It is hoped', the German prose stated drily, 'that they will be of interest and of help in understanding your great uncle's life and times'.

Stewart grunted to himself as he read these lines.

He looked through the items in the parcel. There were diaries. Lots of them. Stewart examined the dates. Most covered the fifties, when the rebuilding was taking place, but at least one seemed to be from the war years. There were photographs, Werner at school, Werner in the army. Relaxed, surrounded by friends. A few were of the rubble of some bombed city. Then, from later, his wife, looking pretty, happy. His first shop, Werner's name above the door. Another, a picture of Werner and two other men, all three smiling, business associates perhaps, arms on each other's shoulders. The handwritten date on the back was 1955. There was a medal, no inscription or date, it was unclear what it was for, or who might have presented it. A cigarette case, coins, a watch.

He picked up a sheaf of papers bound by string and enclosed with a loosely tied hard cover.

He looked at the first few pages. The sheets were yellowing, the corners frayed and torn, the pages were covered with lines and lines of handwritten notes. There was a date on the first page, November 1947, and a signature. He examined the writing, formal, slightly old-fashioned, but with crossings out, notes in the margin, a few spelling mistakes. The first three or four pages were clearly meant as a kind of introduction, but - to what?

'What I am about to describe will, one hopes, be useful ...', 'What follows ...', 'That which you are about to read ...'

He flipped through. The discursive style persisted. He could see no consistent theme. He sat in reverie for a few seconds,

The Escape

wondering whether he had the time and energy to sift through it all.

The telephone rang.

'Hello'. It was a few seconds before he picked up the receiver.

'Hmm .. Can you make sure you are back home at six thirty this evening, the Nanny can't stay late, and I'm gonna be stuck on a train for ages.'

It amused, and, it had to be said, annoyed him that his wife would launch into a phone conversation, no Hello, no introduction, no How Are You. As if she expected him to have been thinking about her at precisely that moment.

'Jane, hi, err, let me think.' *And how are you?* 'Look, this burglary over the weekend, we've been spending all day trying to patch things up..'

'Yes, I was speaking just now to Dawn. And, hey, by the way, why didn't you tell me earlier?'

He felt a tension creeping over his skin. A hint of confrontation in her voice.

'We've been so busy,' And he described the endless round of meetings he had had that day. He considered how soon he could finish the conversation, while his wife talked of her own schedule, a series of meetings in the north of England. Stewart had planned to take his staff for a beer after work, but that would have to be another time.

'OK, Fine, ' he said finally. *You win.* 'Fine. I'll leave in fifteen minutes.'

'I'll see you this evening, then. Don't wait up , I'll be back late. I'll grab a bite to eat on the train. Love you, love to Ali. Bye'.

Love you too. He put down the phone. When was it, he asked himself, that conversations with his wife became a contest. He wondered whether Alison, just eight, ever noticed it. He was sure she did.

He began to trace back in his mind the history of this tension. Had it been when she started work again? *No, surely not*, he thought to himself, *don't be an arsehole*. He had always supported her shop. Yet this shop that she ran with her business partner seemed to stand between them somehow.

Jane had been a journalist in the fashion world, writing freelance for an endless stream of women's magazines. She had stopped when Alison was born, but by chance met a friend from her University days. It soon became apparent that they shared a secret dream to design, make and sell their own clothes. With no experience, they set about acquiring premises, a small shop in one of the fashionably rundown parts of London, then a pattern cutter and material. They approached contacts in the fashion and entertainment worlds. Then, as if by magic, they found their first collection was successful beyond their dreams. A model from New York, as they both told it later, fell in love with their clothes, one or two upmarket fashion houses bought their items, and the business was up and running. They kept things small, hiring few staff, doing the design themselves, letting word of mouth serve for marketing.

Yet even as her shop prospered - and she was always had an actress or a model or a rock star's girlfriend who was visiting or buying - he began to feel as if the clothes and the shop themselves were a barrier between himself and his wife. He hated the clothes. He had never said this. And he never would. But they did not seem to him attractive, sexy, even practical or hardwearing. They did not even appear to be new. Instead they had a feel that was described to him by his wife as lived-in, and her friends nodded approvingly. The shop itself was - to him - dark, cramped, although she described it as a personal space, comfortable and comforting. She had filled it with decorative items she had picked up travelling, or on her own shopping expeditions. Her friends and her regular customers would turn up as much to talk and chat as to buy. They would stay late into the evening and share a bottle of wine. The conversations they

The Escape

had with each other appeared to him so exclusive in a female way. He sometimes studied them. Close eye contact, one girl talking continuously, the other listening, gaze fixed, on her lips a slight smile, interrupting only to agree with a gesture of physical contact, a hand on an arm. He - and he felt all men - could never understand this mode of communication. It described a world that looked on the surface the same as his own, yet diverged in some strange but fundamental way.

He thought of friends who had been married the same length of time as him, and he guessed that for all of them marriage had become formalised, its passion replaced by a working relationship, a friendship. Was this how it was for everyone? It was as if intimacy followed a worn tramline. Emotional resonance had dried up.

He looked down at Gerhard's package and sighed. He got up from his desk. 'Dawn', he called out. 'I have to go. The cleaners should arrive in half an hour. Explain …' He twirled a finger around in the air. '… all this, make sure - make absolutely sure - they lock up.' He walked around the office, slowly, examining everything. He patted Mike and Bob on the shoulders. 'Guys, you did brilliantly.'

'Stewart, before you go, I assume this is yours.'

Dawn was holding up another sheaf of brownish papers loosely bound. Stewart could see they were similar to the one he had started reading from the package.

'Yes. Yes. That's mine. Thanks.'

He took them from her and looked at the first few pages. More of his great uncle's tight-packed and illegible handwriting.

'Yes, most certainly. These are mine.'

On the first page he noticed a Polish place name. Then a few Russian names. He wondered what connection his great uncle could possibly have had with Eastern Europe.

He walked back to his office, left the folder with the rest of the contents of the parcel, and left the building.

II

'I am just going to get a breath of fresh air.' Stewart got up from his seat, stretched his arms, and walked over to the door. He went through the bank's reception area, out onto the street, and paced slowly up and down the pavement.

He had a yearning to smoke. He had given up cigarettes years ago, but he still enjoyed the occasional cigar, and he craved one now. The feeling of warm smoke brushing against the back of his throat, hovering on the verge of inhalation and slowly being exhaled.

He had been in a meeting with his bank manager and his insurer, and they had decided to take a fifteen minute recess. The meeting had not been going well. The insurance company was raising difficulties with the payout after the burglary, citing deficiencies with the security. The bank was questioning his ability to meet repayments.

Stewart had outlined his requirements for new capital. His bank manager had been non-committal. He talked instead of shifting economic realities, and for a moment Stewart had the crazy fear that he was going to call in the loans straight away. This would kill the company. Dead. Stewart put the idea out of his mind and focused on what he would say when they resumed.

His company had been running six years now, and like his wife's had come about almost by chance when business seemed to walk through the door. He had studied European Languages and Culture at University, and moved effortlessly into business journalism, finding a place on the foreign desk of a financial weekly. He had spells in Paris and Frankfurt, establishing contacts in both cities. Back in London, he was approached by a British company expanding into Europe. He was asked to accompany them on sales presentations in Germany, to provide language support, help with introductions, and general hand

The Escape

holding in a foreign land. Other trips followed, and soon he was taking on staff. He provided language assistance, prepared courses, translated technical documentation. He accompanied them overseas, he arranged meetings with potential partners, prepared intelligence on economic and cultural background. The business grew. Today he was grappling with technology, its threat and its opportunity. He knew that much of what his company did could now be done through the internet and through automatic language translation. Indeed his people made extensive use of these themselves. Would technology put him out of business? Would it open up new avenues to exploit?

Stewart would sometimes force himself to think in German, a language he could slip into as he might do a close fitting suit. His strength, his selling point as he explained to others, was that his personality was neither British nor German. He could think and feel in either language, and it was his German persona he sometimes used to work through problems. He had his mother and her family to thank for this.

She had come to England for the first time at the age of twelve to attend boarding school at her father's insistence. Her own mother was the third child of a family living in the suburbs of Munich. Stewart could hardly remember her, she had died when he was young. She had had two older sisters and a younger brother. Werner. The four of them were young adults during the war, and had all somehow survived, despite Werner being drafted. In the closing months of 1945, Stewart's grandmother started dating a British officer in the occupying forces. Whether it was love, or whether she saw it as the only route out of the devastation of her life at home, or whether it was to escape the memory of the horror she had witnessed, to escape her German-ness, she pursued him and they were married the following year. A daughter followed. They settled in Bonn, her husband happy to pursue his military career overseas. In the late fifties, mindful that the child was growing up without any feeling for the country of his birth, he arranged for her to continue her schooling in England. Stewart's mother remembered this as the most lonely period of her life. Yet, when her father died six years later and her mother begged her to return home, she stayed. It was the sixties, and an endless summer of intoxicating excitement seemed to be dawning in London, which seemed to her the only place in the world she wanted to be. She went to University, fell in love with a lecturer, but cut short her studies when she became pregnant. When Stewart was born, both parents vowed that he should be a child of this new shiny world, not hemmed in by the grey and narrow boundaries of their own childhoods. He learnt English and German as a toddler, spent lengthy spells in Germany with his grandmother, and then, when she died, with his mother's cousins. And also, from time to time, with her uncle. Werner did not always enjoy complete approval from the rest of the family, divorced as he was, without children, his business in manual labour frowned upon, yet it was clear that the young Stewart loved the time he spent with him. Later of course he would discover that his great uncle loved the visits as well.

These were less frequent as Stewart entered his teens. Then, when he was eighteen, his mother died in a car crash. A couple of years later, his father sold his possessions and moved to Spain, to play golf and discuss the life that might have been with other expatriates. For Stewart, once he had mastered the grief of his mother's death, this alone-ness acted as a spur to start living his own life. Marriage, the business, the birth of his daughter all followed.

The business had grown. It was profitable. So why, he asked himself, was he feeling so unsure now, at this point of his life? The break-in had unnerved them all, yet nothing had been taken from the office that was unrecoverable.

His phone sounded. A text. A summons. He smiled. Stewart walked back to rejoin the meeting.

The Escape

An hour later he was in his four wheel drive, heading back to the office, still uncertain what had been decided. Something was not quite right, but he could not identify the source of his unease. He slowed as a traffic jam came up ahead, picked up his phone and rang the office to say he would be arriving shortly. He placed the phone on the passenger seat. Traffic had stopped. He slowly became aware, almost at the threshold of consciousness, of a converging of pedestrians around the cars in the road just ahead. Youths, all youths, he saw trainers, hooded sweatshirts. Their movements were fluid, shouting and whooping percolated down through the muted dinner jazz on the radio. He began to stare at them, unsure what they were up to. He looked on, transfixed, and then knew. They were bending car aerials, sliding keys along doors. He saw a side mirror wrenched off the vehicle two ahead. Suddenly, as if the volume had been turned up to maximum on his hi-fi, a face was pressed against his windscreen and a voice was screaming at him. He gaped at the face, unmoving, something rising up from his stomach. He struggled to hear what the voice was saying. The sounds seemed hardly human. It seemed as if they did not come from the face, now contorted as it pressed closer against the windscreen. Then, a smash from the left, glass spraying over his left cheek. He winced, closed his eyes for a moment and raised a hand to shield himself. The spray settled, he looked up, and two hands were stretching through the broken passenger seat window, grasping at his phone. With one hand he reached down to unbuckle his seat belt, with the other he began grappling with the hands protruding through the window. Then the driver door was being wrenched open - *damn, he had forgotten to lock it* - arms were reaching in, grabbing him by the shoulders, pulling him back. Panic now. This was a carjack. If they dragged him out the car he would be defenceless. He turned to struggle with the assailant at his right, pulling and clawing at the arms round his shoulder. And then the pressure stopped, the two attackers were running off, his phone in the right hand of the boy trailing, a middle finger raised on the left. Like a slow motion wave, other youths flowed round the cars up the road and then round a corner, and were gone. He sat in his car, stunned, unmoving. A few drops of blood trickled down from his nose, then began to congeal. As in a dream a chorus of police sirens rose behind him. He tried to take it in. Drivers getting out of their cars, assessing damage. A woman at the side of his car, repeating something. He turned to look at her, and his attention began to focus.

'Are you all right? You're bleeding. Are you all right?'

He raised a hand to his face, rubbed a finger in the blood. He felt his nose, his lips, his cheeks, as if to verify that he was still whole.

'Yes, I'm fine.'

He stepped out of the car, surveyed the scene around him, then leaned against the roof and waited a few minutes for his composure to return.

Why me, he thought to himself. Twice in two days. *What's going on?*

The police were pulling damaged cars over to the side. Other traffic was directed away. Once again, Stewart found himself giving statements to officers. Someone asked him whether he needed an ambulance.

He had to escape for a moment to think. He found a public phone, called the office again, then, seeing a café, bought a take away espresso and returned to the car. He thought about the last few minutes, and his imagination began to roam in a frenzy. Fantasies crowded through his mind. He saw himself in a lonely alley handing wads of notes to a man in shadow. He saw himself with a long-barrelled metallic object wrapped in cloth, then blasting rows of beer cans on a deserted beach, the sound of gunshots cushioned by the rumbling storm clouds overhead. He imagined himself hunting down his assailants one by one in the backstreets of the city, subjecting them to an implacable and ghastly retribution ....

Snap out of it, he told himself.

He waited half an hour to be released by the police, then, seeing TV cameras arriving - some local station - he decided to get away and sort out the paper work for insurance later. He started the engine, pulled out into the road, and headed towards the office.

III

He sat in his study at home and opened the parcel. He still had not had a chance to go though the contents in detail, and it occurred to him that he should at least phone Gerhard or Marta to say that the package had arrived. It was about ten, Alison asleep, his wife out with friends. Perhaps it was a good thing that he and Jane had an evening apart. The conversation had been difficult at supper the previous night.

Jane had long wanted to open another shop in New York. As soon as Alison left the table Jane explained that she and her partner wanted to go to Manhattan to set up the project. As they cleared the dishes she elaborated her plans, slyly, as if it were all an afterthought, a trifle.

She said how successful the shop was becoming in London, and how much she enjoyed running the business.

'We've had so much interest from New York. They've been telling us we've got to go over there.'

'That's great,' Stewart said. 'But … But do you have to be there to make it happen.'

'Angie's been over a few times, she's met a lot of people. Some of the stores are interested. Yes, I do need to be there. Me as well. To make it happen. You know that.'

Stewart was never totally at ease with Jane's business partner. Angie seemed to Stewart to epitomise the fluff and froth of the fashion industry. When he spoke to her he always asked himself - cruelly - if there was really anybody there. He suspected, for no good reason, that she was gay, and this, absurdly, compounded his unease. No matter how he tried to resist it the feeling, no matter he told himself he was an old fool, he could not help but feel proprietorial about his wife.

'Well …. It sounds great.' *No, it's not great*, he thought. Then he heard himself adding, mechanically, 'I'm not sure how much I could help out financially, but perhaps there would be something to get you started.'

He regretted the statement immediately. It concealed his unease about his own business. His bank manager had come back to him after the meeting to say that there would be no new finance. Worse, because of recent cash flow issues, his company was being put on special watch. Stewart was horrified. Surely the business was sound. And now he felt guilty that he had not discussed any of this with Jane.

She was continuing with her plans, telling him of a local partner they could use, someone who could run the new shop on a day by day basis.

'In fact,' she carried plates into the kitchen, her voice trailing, 'Angie's going out there next week to check out the lie of the land. I want to join her. We think it would take three months to get everything sorted.'

He took a sip of his wine, his mind still with the bank. Then it hit him.

'What?' he spluttered. 'Three months? But, I can't…. you know I can't get away for that long.'

'I didn't mean you should. You wouldn't have to come at all. It's all sorted. We'd be staying with one of Angie's friends, this person has this vast attic somewhere. We can stay for nothing.'

'What about me? What about Alison?' Stewart felt his anger rising. He struggled to suppress it.

The Escape

'Well, I was thinking, the summer holidays are coming. Alison could spend six weeks with me. She would love it. And you can come when you take a summer break.'

'I can't take two weeks off, let alone six. What about us? What about the family?'

'Oh, come on, Stewart. This is not forever. We're not going to move there.' A hint of assertiveness entered her voice. 'This has got to happen. Sometime. Why not now.' She continued, softening. 'Look, I'm sorry. But you know how important this is to me. I've got to give it a try.'

They talked, not quite arguing, all evening. The strain continued next morning as they packed Alison off to school with the nanny. Stewart felt a certain relief when Jane told him she was taking Alison to see her mother the next evening.

Stewart made himself a cup of coffee and returned to the parcel. He picked up the diaries. He knew that one covered the war years. He worked back. Some were from the fifties, the covers of the diaries identical, all the same cheap cardboard material. There was one for nineteen forty-nine, another for forty-seven, then finally - he felt a frisson of excitement - one, battered, stained, a different feel to the hardback cover, with an inscription on the inside. Nineteen forty-three in large letters. He riffled through. The pages for August onwards were missing. He turned to the beginning. There were notes about family life in Munich. They had all celebrated Christmas and New Year, and life was good, despite the war. The second of the three girls was married, and Werner had written a few paragraphs about her and her young children. He wrote of his parents' concern that the oldest had still not found someone. But she enjoyed her work as a teacher in the local school.

Werner was already in the army. He had had Christmas leave, but entries from January onwards began to describe life back in barracks. Soon after, he was off to a camp in the East for training. The language was bizarrely optimistic and relaxed.

There was a series of entries describing a boxing tournament. Werner, it seemed, was a contender.

'22 February. My first fight. Four rounds, three minutes each. I am up against someone from dormitory five. Round three, a hook with my right catches him unawares. What a beauty. He falls, rises after seven. But that's it. A minute later, fight stopped. I win. Second match. This guy is too good, he keeps on coming, I cannot defend. He wins on points. Watch this guy, he's going to go all the way.

'23 February. Finals. My guy's there, loses to a knockout punch, last round. They let us have beer after. We toast the Fuehrer. What a fine day.'

Stewart sensed a kind of misplaced euphoria.

The entries following were barely legible, but as he struggled to piece together the narrative it became apparent that Werner was back from training. Quickly, the tone shifted, the mood was more sombre. The gaps said it all. Names and places were left blank, or designated by letter only. One sensed the threat of the censor. There was, perhaps foolishly it seemed to Stewart, a mention of an enemy bombing raid close by the barracks, then, the next day, conflicting rumours on the progress of the war. Some whispered all was not good.

He and his companions were waiting to be posted, somewhere on the Eastern front. Then, one day, a long journey.

'1 April. 5.00 Lorry ride to the station, boarded train. 7.30 Departed. We are heading East to P... The train rumbles along all day. Many stops. The land here is flat, monotonous. There are no cars, except for army vehicles. People are primitive. Friendly though.'

'2 April. Still on train. Joined by men from other regiments. They've seen action on the front; back for short break, now returning. They love scaring us with their stories. The enemy is barbaric; everything they told us in school about the Bolsheviks is true. We all feel we must keep our resolve, no matter what. As long as we stick together. Passed a town today. Or we think it

The Escape

was a town. All buildings in ruins. The people like animals. Tomorrow we arrive at our new camp.'

He repeats the scare stories the veterans use to intimidate the new recruits. Werner and his friends are unnerved.

Stewart continued to read.

Werner's arrival at a new camp, then - his first posting - to battle. And here Stewart had to take a break. To think. Take a leak. Quite suddenly he was sweating. He walked to the drinks cabinet in the living room and returned with a bottle of Scotch.

The soldiers are posted a few miles behind the front where they can provide logistical support and man the reserve artillery.

There are bombardments, from Werner's side and from the enemy. German airforce planes head East in waves.

One day, a column of prisoners of war arrives. They are bedraggled and undisciplined, uniforms shoddy, unkempt, many with no shoes. Werner and his comrades are contemptuous.

Two months later, his unit is moved closer to the front. Entries are less frequent, the tone is terse.

Later still. They are there. At the front. They see action. A close friend is killed just yards from him. There is a hardness in the writing. He talks of body counts, ambushes, human wave attacks. The reality of war becomes commonplace.

The months of June and July are witness to a deepening nightmare. Then, nothing. August has been torn out. The rest of the year is gone.

Stewart rose from his chair, stretched. His shirt was tight to the skin with sweat. But he felt curiously deflated by the break in the narrative. What happened? Werner had survived the war. He knew that. Had he been injured? Taken prisoner?

Stewart picked up the other diaries. They returned to his life after the war, and there was very little direct mention of the conflict. They described the catastrophe of total defeat. The military occupation, shortages, rebuilding. Fascinating enough, yet Stewart felt a hunger to know the fine detail of what had happened in the critical years. He turned to the two volumes of loose pages which Dawn had found after the break-in. He picked up the first and started reading. There was no date, but it became apparent from clues - events described, names of politicians - all this was confirmed as Stewart consulted websites on the history of the period - that it had been written around ninety forty-seven. This part of the record began as a confession. Werner had something he needed to tell, something he needed to lay down as a permanent record. Some clumsy soul searching, words addressed to a hypothetical reader, a plea for understanding. Somehow it all seemed slightly pathetic. Then, suddenly, the narrative was back in nineteen forty-four. The front line.

Stewart read on.

And on. For six hours. He did not stop until four in the morning. The following day, Friday, he finished work early, left his wife and his daughter to themselves with Jane's mother, and returned to his study to read again all night. He spent the whole weekend working through the two volumes, once, and then, starting from the beginning, once more.

Progress was always slow. The writing was barely legible, the grammar archaic. Odd pages were missing, other pages faded with age. But with any setback, any break, Stewart read, then cross-referenced, referred to textbooks, on his shelf, on the internet, and then re-read. Gradually a narrative emerged. He studied the few photographs in minute detail, he returned to earlier entries, he re-read whole sections in the manuscript he had already covered. He consulted maps, text books. The story took shape, in stops and starts, slowly, slowly. But as Saturday became Sunday Werner's war stuttered back to life.

Once, early on, the phone rang. Stewart counted five, ten, fifteen rings. It stopped. He pulled out the cord.

The Escape

Part Two

I

November, nineteen forty four.
Nine o'clock, a cold morning. Eastern Poland.

Werner came out of his bunker to survey the country around him. He stumbled around for a few minutes, greeting colleagues, sniffing the cold, searching the skies, searching he knew not what for. He glanced over to his right where men were chatting, stamping their feet in the mud, and laughing at some grim joke. He did not recognise these men, but this did not surprise him. He knew that his own regiment, depleted by the losses of the last retreat, was being merged with another. Around him were tens of thousands of men, artillery units, tanks, infantry, all being gathered for another push against the juggernaut of the Soviet forces. Whole armies, including units of the SS divisions, notorious even amongst his own men for their savagery. Yet these armies were, he knew, just the remnants of immeasurably vaster armies which had washed over the far reaches of the East, but which had inexorably broken and rolled back as they fell against what seemed the limitless hordes of the communist fanatics. But his regiment's officers presented them with a very different story. Here, their officers asserted, was the massed concentration of the very best of their country's armed forces, men whose characters were hardened by combat, men who would never surrender, men who were invincible. They would have at their service the very finest examples of German genius: technology, tanks, heavy machine guns, artillery. A re-equipped air force would take the fight back to the Bolsheviks, with waves of fighters and bombers powered by new devices so secret that no details were being released.

Werner himself had watched lines of trucks converging from North and South, he had seen trains with troops arriving from the West. The numbers were swelling, it made him feel once more a spasm of pride and confidence, emotions that had evaporated slowly over the year just gone as news came in of successive defeats. He wondered whether the tide could be reversed. The numbers were impressive, the confidence amongst the officers seemed genuine, yet he could not but notice that so many of the troops arriving from other fronts were more exhausted than battle hardened. So many were bandaged, some were unsteady on their feet, carrying he knew not what kind of wounds, while the troops pulling in from the West included boys and old men. In his bunk, at night, Werner asked himself how these people could form an army fit for combat.

Snow fell. The cold was terrible, it had started to snow a week ago and had hardly stopped. It lent no beauty to the devastated landscape around them. The flakes themselves seemed grey, blighted by the by-products of war, and as soon as the snow fell, it was churned over, muddied, blackened by the constant trampling of feet or the tracks of tanks and armoured cars. Yet he realised, as did every soldier around him, that the snow afforded them an opportunity, as it had halted the advance, at least for the moment, of their foe. They had a few precious days in which to recover their poise and re-group. Their officers were not yet providing them with the fine detail of the counter-offensive, for they knew that Russian snatch squads, operating at night sometimes right up to their own lines, would kidnap lone soldiers. It had to be assumed that these captured men would tell all. Every man could be broken. Eventually. They were never seen again.

Werner recalled the events of the eighteen months past, the days soon after he was drafted, a time of a simple optimism, then successive movements east and further east, as he came closer and closer to the front. He could remember the terrible devastation he had seen in the Polish and Russian hinterland, the scarred countryside, the towns reduced to rubble, buildings laid out in hellish zoned templates of cities as they might have

The Escape

looked years before. Villages emptied of people, ominous pyres burning slowly on the outskirts. Yet the real horror that began to gnaw at him was that all this was not the result of Asiatic barbarism. It was his own people. His own army.

How had he endured the winter of forty-three. The snow, the fog, the mud, the rain. The difficulty of keeping weapons of war working in the cold, yet the terror of the consequences should those weapons fail. He remembered a column of men who had escaped from Stalingrad. Their eyes were empty as they described a whole army which had fought to a standstill then been encircled by the enemy, and had finally capitulated there, abandoned now to endure a fate beyond imagining. He recalled his fear as the spectre of close combat came nearer, then the sense of dreadful relief as it arrived and he survived. Then a slow retreat as German forces began to buckle. There would follow a period of thrust and counter thrust. But the overall direction of their movement was retreat. A loss of morale threatened to engulf the remaining armies in the summer, when news of the setbacks on the Western front began to trickle through, but somehow they had managed to hold on to what they still had, and to prepare for one final push against their enemy.

They waited as the build-up continued. Werner sometimes asked himself how all these people could have arrived at this moment in time, this impossible collision between these vast armies. He thought back to his school days, he saw himself as an eleven year old. Images came to him of rote learning poetry in school, of stern lessons in the rudiments of algebra. He thought of his family, of the village he grew up in, his friends, the streets of the nearby town, the sense of order and the rightness of the community he had been nurtured by. He recalled his father talking about the despair of the years after the last war, when Germany seemed to be sinking into chaos. His father had a visceral fear of the Bolshevik, and Werner could visualise him lecturing his mother on what would happen were the country to fall to them. All this would be lost, he would say, as she served supper for the family; our jobs, our community, the family, the food we are eating. The sense of order, an order which means we know where we stand, so we can get up in the morning and feel confident about the day ahead. That sense of order, Werner thought. Yes, that was it, that was the structure that gave their lives meaning, that kept anarchy at bay. That was something worth fighting for. And how they had all listened when a charismatic leader arose to tell them that that sense of order was what made the German people great, and that it was their God-given duty to spread this order across Europe and to the far reaches of the East.

Werner looked around him. He knew now that it was that order that had now been destroyed by this war, to be replaced by shattered towns, burnt villages, desperate peoples roaming across frontierless lands in search of shelter and food, trying to avoid two great armies as they grappled with each other in a fight to the death. This order, this thing they had tried to take to the world, had instead been obliterated from this world.

The Reich was to last a thousand years. Instead, Werner feared, it was the chaos of this wasteland that would last a thousand years.

February, nineteen forty five.

A battle. A counter-strike. A defeat. Capture.

Hundreds of them, more joining each day. They had been stripped of weapons, of their papers and other possessions. Russian guards surrounded them, arrogant, swaggering, screaming abuse. Try to escape, they signalled, and if you are not shot you will die of the cold. Some had had their coats taken, others their boots. Many of the prisoners looked ready for death. Many did die. Some had dreadful wounds, care was minimal, others succumbed to cold and malnutrition. The dead were piled into mass graves dug by the prisoners. Yet numbers continued to grow, as more and more prisoners arrived.

The Escape

The German fight back had started in early December, when a break in the weather gave them an opportunity to move quickly across ground. Armies began to move East, then to split North and South to counter the waves coming in across the many borders with Russia and its satellite states. The enemy was initially taken by surprise and began to fall back along a stretch of fronts. The concentration of German armour proved decisive, it seemed so long since they had been able to amass this number of tanks, and it remained true that nothing the Russians had could match a *Königstiger* in a shooting contest. Moreover, the Germans had learnt from their enemies in being able to bring to the battlefield the brute cunning and the toughness in close quarter combat that the Russians had always had in the great battles of earlier years. For a few weeks, progress was swift, and their enemies fell back in all places. But the Russians had also learnt from their adversaries, and were able to bring concentrated air power to bear on the Germans. In vain did Werner and his comrades look for the overwhelming air support they had been promised, and which they had taken for granted in earlier years. A column of men linking the front line to their reinforcements was wiped out in an air strike, and the forward momentum began to stall. Christmas and New Year came and went, and Werner's division found that it had to pull back to a town they had themselves retaken only a few days before. They dug in, but this tactic turned out to be a serious error, as they found themselves surrounded and cut off. Days of ceaseless artillery pounding followed, with raids by Soviet troops at night into the town itself, incursions which were bloodily beaten off. One of the remaining senior officers was asked to attempt a breakout. A detachment of troops was pulled together, and under cover of darkness they tried to punch a way out to the West. A fearsome firefight was heard on the edge of town all night, but by daylight a quietness descended on the battle zone. They feared the worst.

The barrage resumed later. Food and ammunition ran low. The commanding officer was shot dead by a sniper, and the will to resist collapsed. Russian troops were openly entering the town during daylight hours, and German units, leaderless, began to lose communication with each other and drift apart as key streets and buildings were taken. White flags appeared over the town as individual groups attempted to surrender. Many were shot where they stood, but as the fighting slowed more and more German troops gave up the struggle. By the end of the day the battle was over.

For Werner and the remains of his regiment the nightmare began. A forced march eastwards, every day filled with the same unintelligible commands, the same rifle butts in the back, the same fear that to stop or to slip back would be met, as it was for many, by a shot to the head. Three days later they arrived in a makeshift camp, with prisoners of war already erecting a fence around a barren field. The camp became their home for the next few weeks.

Werner began to spend his time in the company of another soldier with whom he had trained from the early days. Hans had been through the first experience of combat with Werner. They had been separated when the Soviet counter-offensive began, and Werner almost failed to recognise him now, emaciated, his hair thinning. They exchanged stories when they had a few moments together, and then they swapped soup or scraps of bread. For both, this human contact became the only thing of any worth in their lives, and they spent every moment side by side. Some days they worked, digging ditches, erecting buildings and fences. Other days they did nothing. They sat for hours on end in the cold outside, ordered by their guards not to move on pain of being shot.

One day, three aircraft were spotted coming from the West. Old hands could tell by the sound of the engines they were German, and a cheer arose amongst the prisoners, quelled by the guards with shots in the air. The elation turned to doubt,

The Escape

and then dismay, as the planes swept low and started strafing the open areas of the camp. The guards' authority evaporated in an instant, and men were running towards their makeshift barracks when an explosion destroyed one of the buildings. The stream of men heading for cover now broke up and ran in all directions away from the focus of the last burst of fire. The guards shot randomly at the planes, and then, seeing that the panic of the prisoners was turning into a breakout, began firing over the heads of the prisoners, and then right at them. Suddenly the planes were rising and turning away from camp. Perhaps the pilots had realised theirs was friendly fire. Perhaps they no longer cared either way. The panic on the ground intensified as prisoners immediately saw an escape opportunity. The gunfire from the guards increased, reinforcements arrived as two were overpowered and their guns taken. Men scaled the fences. Many were shot clinging to the wire. The tide began to turn against the prisoners. Dogs arrived, and hunted down the few who had scaled the fence. The two Germans with the guns were shot dead. The gates were sealed off with a mass of troops, guards began to advance on the prisoners. The running petered out, they saw the futility of their efforts and sat down where they stood. Calm returned to the camp. Two hours later, the soldiers with dogs returned. They threw down twitching carcasses of two bloodied prisoners. They were hanged an hour later. The next day, they had orders to move further East once more.

Four days later they were in another camp. They had marched some of the time, a line of bedraggled men, some tied together, some stumbling with tiredness or their wounds. At other times they were transported by lorry, the men pressed and forced in, line after line, each vehicle sagging under the weight.

It began to snow, the cold intensified. The new camp was larger, with more men, the security more organised, with lookout towers, spot lights, and guards with dogs. However, the barracks offered some shelter, and the crowding and crammed bodies afforded a measure of warmth. Men continued to arrive, and Werner and Hans began to hear news from the other theatres of war. All of it was bad. The Eastern front appeared to have collapsed entirely. Russian armies had stormed through Poland and had crossed into Germany. Rumours spoke of them on the outskirts of Berlin itself. Someone said that the Red Flag had been raised above the Reichstag. Partisans in Rumania, Yugoslavia, Greece, equipped with foreign weapons, were now fighting openly. German armies were in retreat. In the West, the position was worse. Despair settled over the prisoners. The desire to escape evaporated - where could they flee? What was there left to return to?

Werner and Hans found themselves seeing more of a young officer whose bunk lay next to theirs. The separation between the officer class and the men was gone. Werner guessed this was in part an attempt by their jailers to humiliate the officers. But military discipline had broken down anyway. At first the officer said nothing, he sat on his own in the courtyard, knees drawn up to his chest, head lolling about. And then, days of eating together, sharing what scraps they were given, he began to open up. Christoph had seen action on the Eastern front, but right at the beginning, when the German army had stormed across Poland and the Ukraine, and nothing seemed able to stand in their path. In those euphoric first weeks, they had talked of annihilating the Soviet empire by the end of nineteen forty one. He had studied Russian history at university, he described how he had been so taken by the scope of this modern day German victory that he could not but see their success as a historic move to sweep away centuries of Russian backwardness and oppression. A posting to France followed - he sighed as he recalled a different kind of life, where even as an occupier it was possible to catch a glimpse of culture and refinement - but then, as the flow of battle began to turn, he was recalled to his old unit in the East.

The Escape

He began to talk about the history he had studied, the long pattern of tension between East and West, and how he had believed in the need to spread the German enlightenment to all parts of the world. By force if necessary. He had looked away when a terrible destruction had been laid upon the conquered territories by the more ardent senior officers. The end justified the means, they said. But the end was this, that they had run up against the barrier of a brute, Asiatic monster which now threatened the West itself.

'I tell you,' he warned. 'It will be bad. Very bad. And the further East they take us, the less likely we will ever return to civilisation.'

He told them of rumours that had reached the West of vast camps stretched out over the far northern parts of Russia, where men laboured in slave conditions in permanent winter.

'England, France. These countries are finished, they are nothing. The Americans, who knows. Perhaps they might strike a deal with the Soviets. But I tell you, if we get sent East, we are dead.'

Werner and Hans had never consciously considered what might happen when hostilities ended. But they knew suddenly, in their hearts, that the German cause was lost, and then they knew something else, that they had taken for granted that with the war ending, as in some sporting contest or game of skill or chance, they would walk away once it was over, and would be allowed to drift back to their towns and villages. Now, for the first time they began to question whether this could happen at all. And if this did not, where would they end up? What would happen to them?

II

The weeks passed.

March came, the cold continued. One day they were told to assemble in the main courtyard. There were by now thousands of prisoners in the camp and it took an hour for them to march out, block by block, line by line. The start was delayed further when it was decided that the sick had to be carried from their beds and brought outside to hear the announcement. A loudspeaker system was set up, and, with scores of guards surrounding, a Red Army officer made a short speech in Russian. He finished abruptly and walked away. A translation was read by one of his juniors. At first light the following morning they were to assemble again at the same spot. Lorries would take them to a nearby rail crossing, where they would board trains to transport them to a new camp. No more information was given. A murmur started up amongst the prisoners, but this ended instantly after a few shots in the air from the guards. They were told to disperse, the prisoners waiting till they had returned to their barracks before they started chattering amongst themselves.

Werner had felt a moment of hope. Could this be it? Perhaps the war had ended and they were going home. Hans said this was the most likely explanation. After all, if it was all over, surely the guards themselves would want to get back to their families. They would not want to spend the rest of their lives looking after a few Germans. Christoph, meeting them later, had a different view.

'You will not be going home. They want their revenge. We will go East.'

Werner and Hans refused to believe him. By seven the next morning convoys of trucks had already taken them to a rail siding where the train waited. A long line of wooden carriages stretched behind the locomotive, and the prisoners were herded in, from the front carriage to the rear. Inside, no seats or benches of any kind. Wooden floors, wooden slats for walls. Cars were filled to bursting, one after the other. Werner, Hans and Christoph, amongst the first to board their carriage, tried to carve out some space for themselves, but soon had to abandon this as more and more prisoners were crammed in with them.

The Escape

Their carriage full, a massive door was slammed shut, and chains and padlocks secured. The hours passed, they could hear lorries continuing to arrive, and shouts and screams as more carriages were filled. An agony of expectation descended on Werner as he tried to guess which way they were heading. Some of the men peered through slats at the land and the sky around them, trying to get bearings, trying to figure out the direction in which the train pointed. Others who had fought campaigns in this region and knew of this rail line had already guessed. Rumours spread through the carriage. All that remained was for them to start moving.

The sound of lorry engines ceased. Someone shouted out that a few Germans still stood on the grass beside the railway line. There was a sound of padlocks being unhinged. Their door was re-opened, and half a dozen more prisoners were thrown in. They heard this repeated up and down the line as the final men were loaded onto the train.

A sound of an engine powering up, blasts of steam, a few sudden judders, metal grinding and stretching, and the train began to move off. A low moan arose from the prisoners. Their hopes were extinguished. After a long, laborious, slow retreat from Russia, they were now heading back there.

Conditions on the train started off bad, and got steadily worse. The men had no space of their own, and initially tried to stand, so as to give those around them what room they could, but this became impossible as time passed and men started to tire and cramp. They found themselves squatting, and then they stood and sat down repeatedly just to stretch muscles for a few moments. Some slept standing, those lucky enough to be positioned against a wall used it to support themselves as they dozed. A wind blew through the carriage, the rotting walls giving little protection. At one stop, a group of Russian soldiers, for no reason other than their amusement, doused them with freezing water from a hose pipe. The sick and wounded moaned in a corner, and after the first night, two were dead.

And then Werner and Hans noticed a change coming over Christoph. As if coming back after a period of torment and self-examination, he began to take part in the gossip and the activity around him. They saw a hint of assertiveness in his demeanour, he began to use his status as an officer to take charge. As dawn arrived after the first night, with two corpses in the carriage, it was he who separated the dead from the living, as far as it was possible to do so, and then tried to make a small space for the remaining sick. It was he who negotiated with the Russians to get rid of the bodies when they next stopped.

Later that day, as mess and excrement piling up on the floor threatened a descent into savagery, and after a few fights had started, it was he, with two other officers working alongside, who managed to instil some self-discipline into the men and prevent anarchy.

Days of slow progress followed. There were stops and starts, it was clear that the railway line had been damaged in the war and that work was still going on to repair it. They stopped every morning to dispose of those who had died overnight. They passed the occasional station, where bread and water might be taken on board and handed around. Sometimes they stopped for no reason anyone could see, once when they heard a massive fleet of planes passing overhead. Werner recalled the bombing by their own airforce when they were in the camp, and a cold sweat passed over him as he wondered whether the same would happen here. But this time the planes passed on into the distance, and the train moved on. At other times, they stopped and the men from one or two of the carriages were let out for fifteen minutes to walk around, while their guards, heavily armed, chatted and smoked. The first time this happened, to the carriage just in front of them, Werner noticed Christoph and the other officers watching by the door, mouths open, their faces grey. When their turn came, the officers were the last to leave the carriage. Christoph would tell them afterwards he was expecting every man to be shot. The officers had hesitated but decided eventually it would be better not to draw attention to themselves by remaining on the train.

Werner and Hans now spoke less frequently to Christoph. He spent more time with the other officers who all began to sit apart from the troops. But on one occasion he squatted down at their side and remained with them for a while. His mood had reverted back to an introverted melancholy.

'You know we are heading further into Russia,' he told them. 'This is going to be the end of us. Unless we do something now. We will die in their camps, and our story will never be told.' And then, to himself, 'How did it ever come to this. How.' But a moment later he answered his own question. 'Of course, we made it happen this way. This is our legacy. This cursed state is our own creation.'

He stayed with them for thirty minutes. But later, they saw him back with his fellow officers. He seemed chattier, once more taking an interest in what was happening around him.

One of the other soldiers squatting next to Werner asked him, 'Why do you speak to him? He can't help anyone. He's not interested in us. Stick with your own kind.'

But Werner said, 'Listen to what he's saying. He knows the Russians. He knows what they're like. He knows what they think.'

'It's hopeless,' the soldier said. 'Who cares what he knows?' Werner said nothing.

He began to notice that whenever the train stopped the officers were observing the guards closely. After the doors were slammed shut, he saw them once or twice scratching figures on one of the wooden slats with a loose piece of metal, it seemed at a distance like numbers, or times of day. It came to him they were recording the guards' comings and goings and how many they were. He saw the officers in long conversation with one of the men who had worked on this same railway line, years ago when the surrounding land had been occupied by the German army and the line had been used to transport men and machines to the front.

And he himself began to observe.

When they left the last camp they had taken on two carriage loads of guards, one at the front, another at the rear. Initially, there had been more stationed on the roofs of each carriage, but this had dropped off after a while. He rarely heard their voices or footsteps on top of his own carriage. At each stop, the guards would fan out alongside the train. Then, guns at the ready, they would wait for three or four among them to unlock the padlocks on a carriage door and let the prisoners out. The prisoners, cramped, gasping for air, would stagger out, more often than not falling in a heap on the ground for minutes until they recovered. At stations, there were extra guards, as the soldiers manning the station would join in the marshalling of the Germans. But elsewhere, away from the official stops, Werner noticed fewer and fewer guards actually coming out of their carriages to oversee the prisoners' exercise. Perhaps they felt that malnutrition and sickness would do more than anything else to keep the men quiet. Werner watched and he counted. One night he heard Christoph whispering in his ear, and then something was casually passed into his hand. He felt a cold metallic object. He hid it down his trousers. Taking a peek as dawn came, he saw a nine inch bolt, rusted but intact, recovered from where, he could not guess. It had been crudely sharpened. A quiet expectation settled on the prisoners during the day. It became apparent that officers were taking turns to move about in the carriage, slowly, edging past one man after another, talking, asking them how they were holding up, where they had been captured, what regiments they had served in. When Christoph approached Werner and Hans, the two of them sensed a purposefulness they had not seen in him since first meeting in the camp weeks ago.

The Escape

'Our opportunity will come soon,' he whispered. 'We must not waste it.'

The day passed. In the afternoon they stopped at a primitive station, a wooden siding with a shack. A few soldiers were billeted there. They helped the train guards distribute some bread, passing or sometimes throwing loaves through the slats of the carriage doors. After half an hour the men in the carriage just ahead of them were let out for fifteen minutes, the station guards staring over them, rifles ready. Half an hour later, the train was moving again, but no faster than at a horse's trot. Daylight would soon begin to fade. The train slowed, then stopped, as it had done so frequently over the last few days, in an empty, flat plain. There was no reason given, no indication of when they might once more be in motion. After twenty minutes they could hear guards walking down the length of the train. They walked past, walked back, shouting, laughing amongst themselves. One of them barked out commands, and soldiers began to unlock the door of their carriage. The prisoners were to be given a few moments to stretch, and as usual they tumbled out of the door, a mass of human flesh slowly expelled from the carriage. Once Werner had recovered his breath, he looked around him. Grey, featureless plains stretched away to the horizon with no trace of human life. As ever, guards surrounded them, but Werner noticed almost an air of nonchalance about them. He counted nine, ten, no more. Some had their rifles over their shoulders, two were chatting amongst themselves. Werner knew these men had come from the guard wagon at the front of the train, but the numbers watching over them were so few that he guessed that some had not even bothered to step outside, perhaps because of the cold, perhaps because of a growing apathy amongst their captors. The guards from the rear wagon were nowhere to be seen. Werner saw Christoph and the other German officers in a tight group of about ten, all of them huddling close by the carriage. Spread out in bunches were about forty more prisoners, all stamping their feet up and down, waving their arms about.

And then Christoph approached the guards.

Guns were pointed. He paused, shouted a few words in broken Russian. He repeated what he said in German.

'Bodies. Can we get rid of them? Two more have died.'

Werner looked on, shocked. He had not seen any prisoners looking ill over the last twenty four hours. And bodies were usually disposed of in the morning when the prisoners themselves were forced to dig rough graves in the wasteland beside the track. The Russians looked to their officer. He shrugged and lit a cigarette. Christoph walked back to the carriage door and, with the help of two men, dragged two bodies, one after the other, out of the carriage. They carried them a few yards, then threw them over a snow bank, away from the prisoners and guards. There was no attempt to bury them.

It was dusk. The guards were indicating that the men had to climb back in to the carriage. Two guards began to stroll back to the front. A mass of prisoners moved listlessly towards the carriage door. But the officers and those surrounding them remained still, and they now began to stare at their guards, saying nothing, doing nothing, simply staring. Two guards approached them. They shouted. The men stood still. A rifle butt was raised at one of them. The weapon remained, poised above him. A jerking movement, a powerful blow. The officer's head flopped to one side, the man fell to his knees. He turned his face back up to his attacker. The white skin of his cheek darkened. A patchwork of blood emerged on his right side and trickled down. He climbed unsteadily to his feet, leaned on a man next to him, but otherwise remained unmoving. Two more of the guards closed up on the group of prisoners, another blow hit the officer. He fell again to his knees, and did not get up this time. The guards who had started to walk back to their carriage, now thirty yards away, stopped and turned. Yet they did not walk back. Instead they watched, frozen in time, waiting, expecting, as did everyone, that the officer would be shot. Werner looked on, horrified, an unbearable tension crackling between every observer, a tension waiting to be resolved by a single rifle shot to the head.

Suddenly, men were running, men around the wounded man were rushing at the guards. Three were now so close the guards had no time to fire. They were grappled to the ground. The other guards watching backed off and start firing indiscriminately. Werner saw men fall. And then Christoph was moving amongst the rest of the prisoners, hissing as he passed.

'Now, now, let's take them.'

A roar arose amongst the rest of the men, who moved as a slow mass onto the guards. More shots were fired, but in a moment the guards were within arm's length, and they fell. Werner found himself with three others on top of one of them. The man was screaming as fists and boots fell on him. Werner scrabbled around in his trouser leg for the weapon he had been given, and he began scraping it across the man's neck. Blood sprayed, his screams turned to a paroxysm, and then he was silent.

Werner looked up. Dazed. He saw the two guards who had been watching thirty yards away and they were running towards them but two figures appeared out of the darkness of the bushes beside them and forced them to the ground. The dead men. The corpses. The corpses. Werner suddenly understood. Christoph's plan. The men wrestled, four figures rolling around in the hardened mud. Christoph ran towards them, calling others to help. Two, three, four followed, sprinting towards the fighters. In seconds the Russians were overwhelmed.

A howl rose from the prisoners in the next carriage, and then the next, as men strained to see through the slats of the doors.

Guards streamed out of their wagons at front and rear of the train, but at once they halted and took cover, as a barrage of gunfire from captured weapons was aimed at them. Werner looked around him. Their own guards were dead. He saw a dozen Germans lying face down, unmoving. Casualties of the initial charge. The officer who had been beaten was sitting at the side of the train, head still bleeding. Another man wrapped cloth around him.

Christoph took charge. He ordered two soldiers to find the keys for the carriage doors, he ordered two others with a captured rifle to shoot open another carriage. Within thirty seconds the men from carriages ahead and behind were streaming out. Then Christoph took a troop of a dozen or so men, handed guns to a couple, and crossed under the train to the other side, where they sprinted forward. The rest of the men, now a hundred strong, the total rising as other carriages were opened, began to move on the guards at the front. Gunfire assailed them from front and rear, progress was slow as they crouched, took what shelter they could in the bushes at the side. They heard the Russians behind them moving forward, so they pushed on ahead themselves, the half dozen men with guns providing some cover. And then they saw the guards ahead of them themselves being attacked from the rear as Christoph's men came round the other side of the train, and they broke into a trot and then a run towards the front carriage. Half a dozen fell. Then they were amongst the Russians and sheer force of numbers overwhelmed them. Some tried to clamber back onto their carriage and they were shot in the back by their own weapons. In seconds it was over. More guns were handed out, and they turned to hold off the advancing troops from the rear. Christoph dispatched six men to the engine. The drivers, cowering, were overpowered.

Men were now sent around the other side of the train to come up from behind. Others were ordered to climb onto the roof of the leading carriage and work their way backwards. The

The Escape

remaining Russian guards found themselves fighting in three directions. Bodies fell, there was no cover for them, and slowly, slowly they backed away from the train towards bushes at the side. Visibility was beginning to fade, and abruptly, with a final, sadistic volley of bullets into one of the carriages which had not yet been opened, they faded away into the landscape behind them.

'Hunt them down,' one of the officers shouted, and a group of men started after them. They heard shots, but twenty minutes later the men returned. It was too dark, they had caught a few, but others had escaped and they could no longer follow the tracks.

All the carriage doors were now unlocked, and men streamed out to experience their first unrestricted movement in months. Guns and food, medicine and coats were retrieved from the guard wagons and collected by the front carriage. A meeting was called, and the men, five, six, seven hundred strong, gathered in a tight mass. A group of senior officers climbed aboard a carriage, and addressed the men from the open doorway. They had a decision to make, a decision which they had to make immediately. Guards had escaped, they would raise the alarm. Perhaps it had already been raised. All the men wanted to head west, even though they could not guess what they might find there. But they had to decide how. They had the train. Should they reverse it, head back the way they had come, as far as they could go? Or should they abandon it now and travel by foot? The officers recommended that they leave the train at once, it was far too conspicuous, but it was clear that a number of the men wished to remain with it. There were engineers amongst them, they had the captive drivers, they could get it to run in the opposite direction. They said they should take it as far as they could go, get some distance between themselves and the east, and only then abandon it to continue on foot. Some of the officers tried to dissuade them. They would be an easy target for bombers, for enemy soldiers hunting them down. But, whether through exhaustion or a half-sensed resignation to their fate, these men were insistent. They had shelter, they had warmth. They would stay within the confines of the same carriages they had endured for the last four days.

A plan was agreed. The men would split, some staying with the train, others leaving at once. Guns and food were distributed as fairly as was possible, and the men travelling on foot prepared to depart. It was decided to group them in troops of ten. To travel in one mass of three or four hundred would attract too much attention. The groups would travel independently, and they were told to expect they would lose track of each other within the first day.

They were given advice. Travel light. Travel at night. Avoid confrontation, live off the land. Head West, the officers said, keep that uppermost in your mind, never deviate. A couple of soldiers who were familiar with the region from before the war stood up to brief them on towns, roads, rivers.

The senior officer then wished them well.

'God be with you. Who knows, we may yet meet again in Germany. Whatever may have become of it.'

And some of the men boarded the train once more, while others began to fan out, to the north and south away from the railway line.

Werner and Hans were leaving on foot, and found themselves in a group of eleven. Christoph was the only officer. They had two rifles and a pistol. Enough food for a day, some army overcoats. Their plan was to head south during the night, make as much distance as they could between themselves and the train, and then bear round to the west. It was about nine o'clock, and they started off at a trot over dark, barren fields. They were aware, when the clouds parted and a partial moon shone through, that bands of men were passing like shadows around them, but, as the hours passed, they sensed more and more that they were alone, and for the first time in an age, an

The Escape

optimism, a flickering sense that he was in control of his destiny, settled over Werner's mind.

After a few hours, they rested for ten minutes, then headed off again, at a brisk walking pace. They continued, marching, trotting, resting, heading south, then south-west, then west. They reached a road. Deserted. They decided to risk a few hours travelling on it, at least until the sun rose. Then, as the first daylight began to appear, they stepped off the road and headed for a wooded area nearby. As weak sunlight spread out over them, they found cover, and prepared to sleep for a few hours.

They took turns to stand guard, two men at a time serving three hour watches. But when they came to wake the men after the second watch, they found one of them was dead. Christoph touched his cheeks. They were frozen solid. His body had given out after everything it had been through. They deliberated as to what to do with the body. They decided to strip it of all clothes, they could use an extra coat. One man took his watch, itself plundered from a Russian guard less than twenty four hours earlier. They then covered it as best they could under branches, mud and slush, and, as darkness fell, they prepared to move on.

During the day the men on watch had seen lorries and soldiers passing down the road, and they decided that they should stay off it. They needed to follow the direction it was taking, so they walked twenty yards away, ready to move off into the cover of the bushes and nearby scrubland if traffic passed. Twice they heard vehicles, and both times, they paused, hid themselves in the undergrowth, lay flat on the ground, and waited. Convoys of lorries passed by, the second time, as they could see from the beams of weak, yellowish headlamps, loaded with troops. Hours later a tremendous artillery barrage opened up in the far north, and for a while they watched the night sky lit up as successive waves of shells pounded some distant target. But they felt strangely reassured, as they knew this meant that troops were being diverted away from them. For this was their hope, that the war on the front and the demands on enemy manpower would offer them some chance of avoiding discovery, at least until they got closer to Germany.

Hours later, a dog started barking in the distance, and then another. They realised they were approaching a village. They knew it was too risky to walk straight through, so they decided to work their way around it. They moved further off the road. Another dog, a third, started barking nearby. They could make out the faint outlines of houses close to them. They paused. But they knew they could not stop or wait for more light. They had no option. They had to move on. They retraced their steps, then turned off into woodland nearby. Two hours later, they seemed to be clear of the village. They had lost track of the road. The light afforded by the moon and stars was just sufficient to allow them to see fields and grassland stretching ahead of them. They could not waste time searching for the road, so they continued on as best they could. Progress was good throughout the rest of the night. As morning came, and with it mist and drizzle, they looked out and saw that the land was deserted for miles around, and they decided to risk a few hours of daylight travel. By early morning they could make out another village in the distance ahead, and, exhaustion setting in, they decided to find cover and rest for a few hours.

They had a new problem. Food.

The provisions they had taken from the train had almost run out, and there was very little they could scrape off the land, whether by hunting or from the roots and plants they could see around them. Two of the men proposed stealing from the village ahead, and as they argued, Christoph stared into the distance, silent. He then turned and said that they should simply ask the villagers for some food. It did not appear to be a garrison town and they could see no evidence of soldiers or military vehicles ahead of them. They debated amongst themselves whether to ask as Germans or pretend to be Russians. Which would the villagers hate less? It was resolved

The Escape

that Christoph and two others would walk into the village wearing their Russian overcoats and carrying rifles. Using his basic knowledge of Russian, Christoph would ask for whatever the villagers could spare. They would insist that the food was necessary to help the effort to rid the land of the hated fascists. They would do this late afternoon, after they had walked round to the far, western side. Upon their return, they would all immediately start walking as night fell, to put some distance between themselves and the village should the alarm be raised.

They rested for a few hours, and then, as the afternoon came, worked their way to the south of the village and then west, until they found another spot where they could hide and find some shelter. As the time approached, Christoph got up and looked about him, then up at the sky and at the village behind them. He stood still for two minutes. He looked back at the men, nodded at two of them who rose to their feet. The three men began to walk across the mud to the road and then along towards the village. Werner, Hans and the others watched them go and wondered whether they would ever see them again. They had agreed that if the three had not returned by one hour after nightfall, the others would move on. They lay back on the ground and rested as best they could. As daylight started to fade, they saw movement on the road in the distance. They stayed hidden. As the approaching figures got closer they saw them turn off the road, and Werner had a moment of terror when he feared they might be ambushed, but then he heard words hissed in German. Minutes later the three men were among them, clasping each other by the shoulder. The two soldiers with Christoph were jubilant. It had gone exactly as planned. They walked straight into the village, as cocksure as you please. They strode up to the first people they saw, and demanded to see the head man. Christoph had barked a few words in Russian, then spoken some more in heavily accented German as if he was struggling with a second language. Bread, he asked for, cheese, meat, anything you have. There had been an argument, but, as the men told it, those stupid Poles soon capitulated.

Christoph was quiet, however, and told the others to stop bragging.

'They hate us all, these people, they have been trampled on. By us, and now by the Russians. No wonder they cower. Anyway, we need to get moving, they may report this to some real Russians at any moment.'

They walked on for three more hours, then stopped to eat. There was not so much in their haul after all. Some bread, some root vegetables, a small amount of scrawny meat. They ate some, rested for an hour, then moved on to take advantage of the remaining hours of the night.

It continued for five more days. Perhaps six. Werner lost count. Once more, they had to enter a village to ask for food, again disguised as Russian soldiers. Another time they broke into a house at the edge of a village and stole what they could find. One day they saw a massive column of tanks, lorries and troops passing along a road, other times they saw squadrons of planes overhead. The movement was always westward, and they knew that the war could not last much longer. Perversely, the spirits of the men were rising day by day, but Werner worried that they had not met any resistance. It would have to come soon, and then, he asked himself, how would they react? Would they fight? Could they fight? Or would they run?

One more time they prepared to enter a village to get food, and this time Werner, Hans and one other, a dour young soldier called Otmar, accompanied Christoph. They followed the same pattern. The others waited a few miles to the west, they themselves took the road into town mid afternoon. Werner had to control himself from panicking when he saw the first peasants on the outlying huts eyeing them suspiciously. But Christoph did not break stride, he marched on, eyes set straight ahead.

The Escape

'Say nothing,' he whispered to them. 'Let me talk.'

They arrived in a muddy square. Wooden houses stretched up and down, a few carts were parked in the middle, a donkey stood unmoving, head bowed. Some old women on benches, weaving baskets, stopped and stared at them. Christoph went up to them, the others stood at a distance waiting. He shouted words at them in Russian, but they remained unmoving. He switched to German, and his words were accented, unsteady. An old man came sidling into view, and slowly walked up to them. Unshaven, gap-toothed, his clothes torn, he stopped a few yards from Christoph and squinted at him.

Christoph spoke. 'We need bread, food. My soldiers are hungry. Give us what you can spare.'

The old man was silent, then said something in Polish. Christoph waited, then said sharply, 'Deutsch. Deutsch.'

The old man paused again Then he said they had nothing to give. Other soldiers had already taken their food.

Christoph replied, in a softer voice. 'Well give us what you can. We do not ask for much. We need to food to rid your country of the fascists.'

And then Werner heard the faintest whisper of an engine, the sound carried on the wind. He waited a few seconds, alarm growing inside him. Somewhere behind them. He looked at Hans as the metallic rattle, misfiring once or twice, grew louder, and both of them moved closer to Christoph, still negotiating with the villager. Werner tapped him on the shoulder, and he stared back. Werner could see in his eyes that he was frantically pondering whether to stay a few more minutes to try to get something, or whether to leave straight away. Then, soundlessly reaching a collective decision, the four of them were walking away fast, in the opposite direction from the approaching vehicle. The villager was shouting at them. *Deutsche. Deutsche.* They took one last look back, and could see lorries in the distance. They broke into a run, and then saw, to their horror, a Russian soldier emerging from a barn ahead, stretching, rubbing his eyes as if he had been asleep. Then another, then three more. The soldiers looked blankly at the running men, still wearing their Russian overcoats, and suddenly Christoph was shouting words at them in Russian, and pointing back to where they had come from. Werner knew he was trying to bluff his way past them, telling them there were German soldiers behind, but, rather than move in that direction, they began to run alongside, asking questions, pointing, gesticulating, wanting to find out more. Christoph said nothing and faced forward. Werner and Hans increased their pace. Then Werner saw Otmar raising his rifle at the men running alongside, a wild hatred in his eyes. He could see Christoph trying to restrain him, but the man was now shouting in German, pointing his gun at the Russians. Suddenly it was all clear to them. They backed off, but more were beginning to appear, and also lorries behind them at the far end of the road. A shot was fired, then another, and Otmar fell. Werner started to sprint, he ran off the road, jumped a ditch, and scrambled up an incline. He had men after him, and one of his pursuers, throwing himself forward, caught his ankle and caused him to stumble, then fall. Three others were on top of him and he struggled until he was punched on the jaw, and he went limp in an attitude of surrender. They pulled him to his feet and manhandled him back to the road, where two soldiers frisked him, others looking on, rifles ready. They discovered and removed his makeshift blade, then marched him back to the square. Lorries and troops were massing. Minutes later, Hans and Christoph were brought over, their hands on their heads, Hans's forehead bleeding. Otmar's body was dragged towards them. He had been shot in the leg, and was moaning softly. A Russian officer stepped forward, examined the men, then pulled out a pistol, walked over to the injured soldier and shot him twice in the head. The others looked on aghast. This was it. It was over. They had come so close. But they had failed.

But the officer looked at them, shouted something at his second in command, and jumped back in the front compartment of one of the lorries. Orders were barked out, soldiers took out rope, and Werner and the other two others had their hands bound behind their backs. They were bundled into the back of a vehicle. Half an hour later they were moving.

Captives once more.

Another camp, another hell. They had a quick and violent interrogation on the move in the back of the lorry, blows with fist or rifle butt puncturing any pauses. The men had agreed a rough story earlier on - that there were just four of them, they had escaped from a camp two days ago, and had been hiding in the wild since then. They had taken uniforms from dead Russian soldiers at the side of the road. Their captors seemed to accept the story, they were keen to get on. They continued to drive, all afternoon and night, and early the next morning the Germans were handed over at the gates of a compound. Werner looked around him, and from the signs and notices still posted on the gate realised, with a sense of hellish irony, that it had once been a German camp. Used for what purpose then he had no idea. They were taken through the gate, marched over towards a barracks, and told to sit outside until further notice, their hands still tied. That evening, other prisoners, mostly German, a few Poles, returned to the barracks after a day spent working on vegetable patches on the perimeter of the camp. The three new arrivals were untied, and they shared a few scraps of food with the other inmates. Werner found himself talking to one of them who had been a guard at the camp in earlier days when the German army was still sweeping through Eastern Europe.

'We built it, we ran it. That's why it's so well designed. The security is not so good now.'

Werner asked him who had been kept there.

'The usual. Scumbags. Jews. Political prisoners, Russians and Poles, degenerates. But this was a holding camp. No more. From here they went elsewhere.'

And then he added with a smile, 'To other places. And they did not return.'

And now it holds you, Werner thought. *And perhaps you won't return from this one.*

But the man explained it was possible to escape. He knew where the weak links were, two others had broken through the fence the previous night. 'They must have gotten away,' he said. 'They've not been brought back.'

But the next day the men were told to assemble in the courtyard, and from the back of a truck, two men, bloody, barely alive, were dragged out.

A low moan went up from the prisoners. Any hope that escape might be possible was gone.

And then one of the escapees was dragged over to a wooden frame, which Werner saw was a scaffold. There and then, in front of the prisoners, his hands were tied, a wire was attached round his neck, then passed up over the top of the frame, and he was hanged. Werner watched the body, twitching, then slowing in its convulsions and finally swaying in the wind. His spirit seemed to break.

He had fought, he had been captured. He had seen men die, in battle and in captivity. He could endure the pain and discomfort. But he had been unnerved by the conversation about the camp and its onetime use. He knew that many of those labelled undesirable had been rounded up before and during the war, he knew that many Jews had disappeared, he knew about Kristallnacht. But he had always told himself that they had to do this to rebuild Germany and to weed out those who would not support this enterprise. And surely anyone pledging allegiance to the Reich was safe, no matter what their background. He remembered arguments in school, then in the army, where he had fiercely debated these questions again and again, and it came to him now that it had been a sham. A sham to convince himself and himself alone, and to obliterate the doubts which had always eaten away at him. He had seen the

The Escape

destruction that his own people had visited upon Poland and Russia, it had shocked and scared him at first. And then he had taken part in it, he was complicit. It had to be done, they had been told, because the hordes from the East, barely human, would do it to them. He remembered the village where they had been captured two days before, the blankness in the old man's face, a resignation which went beyond fear and hatred, emotions which were futile in the face of two conquerors, German then Russian. Which would they hate less, Christoph had asked at the time, and Werner saw with a new clarity the force of this question. They, the Russians and the Germans, were peoples whose brutality was cut from the same mould. They had been staring at each other across an abyss for years, for decades, for centuries, one waiting to destroy the other. The apocalypse had now arrived, and he was in it, dead centre. He was part of it, he was its agent, caught he did not know how, unable to escape. He looked down at his hands and knew that he himself, with these hands, was somehow responsible, somehow, for the body swaying on a wooden frame a few yards away.

But the road to hell had some way to go. They took the other man away to the guards' area, and he disappeared into the main building. And the prisoners heard the public address crackle into life. And while the prisoners sat in the courtyard, waiting, they heard the recaptured prisoner shouting in terror, then screaming, as his captors set about bit by bit prising his life away from him. For one hour, then two, three, they heard the sounds of beating, grunts in Russian, then the final yells and shrieks, the last frenzy, and the ultimate madness of death approaching. They listened in silence, waiting, seated in the yard, even the guards now silent and subdued. But in Werner's heart, his brief insight into the blackness of his own soul and the sympathy it brought for his victims, and even for his mortal foes, all this began to subside. His humanity ebbed away as the life of the dying prisoner ebbed away, and a hatred re-ignited inside him, subsuming even his fear and terror, and the moment of understanding and empathy was lost in a smouldering loathing of everything and everyone that stood in his path to freedom. He looked over his captors with a bleak gaze. He picked out one, then another, then a third, and his loathing solidified into a cold rock-hard knot of resolve that none of them would stop him in his mission to escape. He continued to stare, silently challenging them, and basked in an icy thrill which coursed through his arms and his body at the challenge that lay ahead.

They were put to work tending the ragged vegetable crops growing on the edge of the camp. Throughout the days that followed, Werner would watch and observe, noting the number of soldiers posted to guard over them, the times of the watch changeovers. He looked at the fences, he took note of the rollcalls, and the cursory manner in which they seemed to be carried out. Evenings, he spoke with Christoph whose desire to escape burned with the same chill flame. He spoke with his newfound colleague who knew the camp in years gone by and understood its secrets. He saw there was a rough shack near the patches where they worked, with a tarpaulin inside, under which men might hide for a few hours. He noted that rollcalls were carried out by numbers, not individual names, and that it would be possible to get men from other work details to cover of an evening when they returned to barracks. From his fellow captive, he learnt of guard changeovers at night, of weak points in the fencing at a spot just a hundred yards from woodland close by. He talked with Hans, who had been through so much with him, but whose will to escape once more was broken. They were barely scraping together a life, Hans told him, their future was empty, but at least they were alive. The time would come when he would return to see the land of his birth. It might be months, it might be years. But it would come.

Werner said nothing. He ignored him and laid his plans.

He contrived to spend a few minutes in the shack by the vegetable patch under the pretence of maintaining his tools, and prepared a spot where they might hide. Two men, Werner and Christoph, would fail to return to barracks one evening. They would hide under a tarpaulin drawn roughly over the floor of the shack. Two inmates, Hans and another, would cover for them during the head count at barracks. The two men would wait for darkness, then, during a slack point in the rounds of the guards during the night, would scale the fence and dash for the woods nearby.

Hans implored them to stay.

'You cannot hide under that tarpaulin for hours, it is too obvious. The guards use the shack for cigarette breaks. For pissing. And you will be spotted when you scale the fence. They have searchlights.'

Werner and Christoph just smiled.

And then something happened.

One morning the men in their barracks were woken an hour early. They were told to assemble outside, their hands were tied behind their backs, and they were bundled into four lorries. There was a forty-five minute journey through a heavily forested area, and they arrived at a town where the Red Army was constructing a fortress. The town had been bombed heavily, and the roads were covered in craters and rubble from collapsed buildings either side. The prisoners were set to work clearing the main street through the town. A day of heavy labour followed. Hundreds of Russian soldiers passed through in trucks, some came on horseback, a few, senior officers, in Mercedes staff cars plundered from the retreating German army. As the afternoon drew on, heavy cloud began to drift over. Later their guards called a stop as light faded and a drizzle began to fall over the town. The men were given bread to eat, their hands were tied behind them, and the guards started to load them back into the lorries. Werner, Hans and Christoph waited in line as the first lorry, then the second, and the third, were loaded with men. They were then bundled into the rear of the fourth, and pushed forward as far as they could go. They squatted on crude wooden benches. The remaining prisoners were forced in behind them, a shuttered metal frame drawn down, and then four guards climbed in to sit at the rear. The convoy moved off as rain began to strengthen. Werner gazed out the back of the truck, and then, straining his neck round, through a tear in the flannel to the front compartment and the road ahead. Their path wound back through the forest, and then began to climb slightly as they skirted a line of hills stretching away to the left. The prisoners listened to the sound of the rain as it intensified against the flannel covering the rear of the truck. A squall hit them. A bank of black cloud came over, the gale appeared to blow up out of nothing and tore through the front and rear compartments of the truck. They could hear sheets of rain coursing down the windscreen. Werner twisted to look through the canvas. The driver slowed as visibility decreased to a few lorry lengths, and a gap opened up between their truck and the others ahead. The road turned, and they entered a stretch which had been cut into a hillside, with a steep embankment leading down to a ditch a few yards off to the right and thick woods beyond. The driver crawled in low gear as the rain intensified. Looking back, Werner saw a small deluge cascading off the road down into the ditch. A black mist came down over them, and then the wheels were jumping up and down over branches of trees lying across the road. The driver stopped. Werner struggled to twist his neck, and looked ahead to see a log blocking the left hand part of the carriageway. The driver extended a hand around an open side window, wiped the windscreen, and began to edge the truck to the right of the roadway to try to work his way round the log. Werner turned back and he and the others looked over to the guards at the rear of their compartment, and beyond them to the sheets of rain which drove against the road and the truck. He could the see the truck turning as it swivelled to the right, and wondered whether they would be unable to pass and forced to stop here. But the truck straightened as they rounded the log, and Werner saw that they were dangerously close to the embankment at the side. He tensed, he expected the lorry to slip away and downwards at any moment. Seconds passed, and the storm increased in intensity.

And then with a jolt the back of the truck was rising, not falling. The truck hung in the air momentarily. Werner had a sense of dislocation, a sense that reality itself was slipping. A crash of thunder stung his ears, then a high pitched whine. Then silence. He was deaf. Another flash of lightning, and he saw two of the guards silently clutching their heads, their fingers bloody. The truck crashed back to the road, its rear end lurching round in a slow, inexorable spin. Smoke drifted into the rear compartment. His hearing began to return, and Christoph was whispering, *A mine, A mine, We've hit a mine.*

And as their view out the back of the truck span slowly and the truck rotated, the driver began to lose control, and the truck, teetering on the edge of the embankment for a few more seconds, began to roll in reverse down the slope. The prisoners watched transfixed as the momentum increased and they saw the ditch at the bottom accelerate towards them. They tried to prepare themselves, to brace themselves, and could not, as the ropes binding them held them rigid against the sides of the truck. The frame of the vehicle shuddered as it picked up speed, and then after a final drop, sheer, vertiginous, the truck crashed against the ground and tore itself apart. The prisoners were thrown towards the rear, metal and rope shearing, men falling one on top of another as the momentum of the mass of bodies was suddenly halted. Metal bent and screamed, the engine roared and then failed, and then there was stillness.

After a few seconds, Werner opened his eyes and willed himself to feel his body, his arms, his legs, his neck, his hands, as if unsure whether everything was still there. He tried to move but found himself on top of a pile of bodies, some writhing, others moaning. But movement was somehow possible and he clambered down slowly, slowly, his hands still tied. He squeezed out from under the awning at the back of the truck, and staggered over to the ground, where he sat dazed. A minute later Christoph joined him, then Hans. A couple of other prisoners emerged. Werner looked back inside, and saw the guards lying in a strange, angular fashion, unmoving, bloody. All dead, some from the mine, others from the fall. He had fallen on top of them. They had saved his life. The guards had saved his life.

He looked at the belt on one of them, and saw a knife. He backed towards the body, drew out the knife, clasped it between his tied hands, and crawled back to Christoph. Facing behind, his head twisted round, he sawed and slashed at the rope at his wrists. Christoph squirmed, stretched his hands free as the rope frayed, and took the knife and released Werner, then Hans. Then he handed the knife over to one of the other prisoners. The rain and wind continued unabated, but now dusk was falling, and light was almost gone. And then Werner and Christoph looked at each other, and a silent communication seemed to lead to one and same thought in their minds. Christoph looked at Hans.

'We're leaving,' he whispered. 'Are you coming?'

In seconds, the three of them were back inside, grabbing rifles, overcoats, belts from the guards. Werner clambered up to see about the driver. He lay in a heap, blood lay spattered over the windscreen. Werner grabbed a knife from his belt, climbed down. The three of them, without a word to any of the other prisoners, turned to start off into the woods. Almost immediately they stopped. Five yards away they saw a figure standing in front of them, upright, in an overcoat. A rifle lay at his feet. A guard. One of the Russians had survived. The three of them stared at him, he stared back. A youth. A boy. His hair was thin and blond, falling over his face, his eyes were bluish, watery. He opened his mouth in a senseless grin, and there were gaps in his greyed teeth, and Werner saw in front of him a farmer's son, a boy who knew nothing about the land he found himself in, who had been dragged over thousands of miles, by people whose motives he could never understand, to serve a terrifying machine bent on destroying an enemy he had never met. A teenager, uneducated, uncomprehending. He continued to beam with his sickly smile, the grin widening. A boy. A fallen angel. The three Germans looked on, caught in a paralysis of indecision as they gazed at the figure in front of them.

And then he dropped to his knees, his coat fell open, and blood began to ooze through his tunic. He continued to stare at them, and raised his hands as if to ask for something. Christoph recovered himself, touched Hans on the shoulder, and they walked past the dying soldier and entered the woods.

Daylight faded, night came, and the storm eased. They were covered in mud, they had no food or water. But they had no ropes binding them, and they could still run. A weak moon afforded them some light, and they guessed a rough direction to follow. As long as it was westward. So they ran on. They ran, and ran, and ran.

Part Three

I

A taxi wound its way through the outskirts of Munich, the driver stopping from time to time to consult a map spread out on the seat beside him. Low cloud hung over the city, and a rain driven by a cold wind covered the streets with a drab grey. As the taxi driver slowed to find a spot to pull over, Stewart stared out the window from the back seat at suburban roads and buildings which seemed to pull weakly at memories from years back. He glanced over at his wife and daughter beside him.

He said in English, 'We'll get there. Eventually.'

The driver, ignoring him, stopped to study the map, then after a while pulled out into the road.

Stewart looked at his wife once more, and this time she caught his eye. 'What's up?'

'Nothing. Just glad you came.'

'So are we,' Jane said. 'Aren't we, Ali?'

Stewart had had trouble sleeping in the days after he read the manuscript. On the third night, as he lay on his side gazing at the moving hands of his alarm clock, he knew suddenly that his wife, unmoving as well, was also awake. He waited a few minutes, wondering whether she would get up for a glass of water. But she lay still.

'Go,' he whispered. 'You must go to New York. I'll miss you terribly. But you must go.' After a while he turned, and she turned as well. He shifted closer to her and nuzzled her ear. 'I know how important this is to you. Take Ali. I'll manage. Somehow.'

She did not reply, but they fell asleep in each other's arms. A week later Angie broke her ankle in a horse riding accident, and suddenly everything had changed. 'It's too soon,' Jane said.

'We're stretching ourselves too thin. We haven't quite figured out what it is we've already got. We'll pick up New York next year.'

Stewart had the impression that when she spoke about discovering what she already had, she also meant her marriage. She had said nothing during the days when Stewart locked himself away with his mysterious parcel. Now, quite suddenly, she was insisting that she finally meet all these Germans she was indirectly related to.

They had been staying at a hotel in the centre of the city for a few days now, and the first evening a party had been arranged for them by Marta. They met other cousins, uncles and aunts, partners and children, most of whom Jane had never met, many of whom she had never even spoken to. Her German was rudimentary, even Alison's was better, yet many of them spoke good English, and she struck up an affinity with Marta, an attractive woman in her early thirties who worked in publishing. Gerhard, formal in a suit, presided over the gathering. Stewart noticed Jane warming even to him, once the children had been put to bed and a bottle of scotch had been opened.

The following afternoon, Stewart had met Marta and Gerhard alone in the hotel. They found a lounge where they could talk, and discussed over coffee the irruption from the past that had landed in their lives. As Stewart laid his briefcase on the table and spread out medals, trinkets and photographs on the table, they talked about the Werner they had known. The Werner they had not known.

Stewart extracted the diaries from his case and then a sheaf of papers on which he had typed up the wartime entries.

'Have you read these?' He asked the two them.

Gerhard looked at Marta for a second, and then back at Stewart.

'Yes,' he replied. 'We did have a look at the diaries before we sent them to you.'

'We were not sure whether it was quite right. You know, having a sneak peek.'

Stewart shook his head. 'Of course it was.'

Marta said, 'I for one am glad you've typed it up. There should be some record of what life was like, for Werner and others like him. Whether we approve or not. You know -' she looked over the papers spread out on the table in front of them. She sighed. '- I should mention that some of the family, especially the older ones, were not happy this material was sent to you. They didn't really know you, they felt this record should have remained here. In Germany. Perhaps it should have remained a secret, just another forgotten record of what it was like in those days.' Marta paused as she dwelt on one of the old photographs. 'There are many in Germany who are uneasy with the narrative that Germans were victims. Don't you think? Gerhard?'

'And there are others,' Gerhard said, 'who think we should just say nothing. Let time, let silence, heal all wounds.' He waited a moment before continuing. 'I remember my grandmother telling me what a shock it was when they discovered Werner was still alive and being held in a British prisoner of war camp. Everyone thought he had died on the Eastern front. No-one ever came back from there.'

'And then a few months later,' said Marta, 'there he was, back in Munich. With some story that he had never seen any action and that his unit, hungry, cold, had surrendered to the first enemy troops they had found.'

Gerhard said, 'He once told me his first hot meal for three months was steak and kidney pie. With potatoes.'

'And carrots,' Marta said. 'Don't forget the carrots.'

Gerhard laughed. 'Carrots. Of course. Your British food. At least it had one fan.'

'He loved your mother. His English niece,' Marta said. 'He really did. Strange in a way. For such a cold man.'

She ran a finger over the cover of one of the manuscripts. 'It's a shock when one is personally implicated in this side of ... what went on. We Germans, we all know what happened. We've seen the documentaries, we've read the books. But when you find out it was one of your own, it ... well ...'

'Do you have any idea what happened to Hans and Christoph?' said Gerhard.

'None,' said Stewart. And then an intuition came to him. 'Unless ...' He spread out the photos on the table like a deck of cards. 'Unless ...' He located the one with the three men, their arms on each other's shoulders. He re-examined the date on the back. 'I wonder. 1955. Do you think ...' He passed it to the others.

'*Waffenbrüder*,' said Gerhard.

'No names,' said Marta, turning it over. 'We'll never know.' Stewart shifted closer and the three of them gazed at the picture.

'Well,' said Stewart leaning back. 'I've got to decide what to do with this stuff. I must say I felt a bit guilty at first. But - guilty about something slightly different. Getting the diaries in the first place. Me. When really it's yours. The family's. Do you think any of you might want it?'

'No. You keep it,' said Gerhard. 'That's what the will said. That's what he wanted.'

'Gerhard's right,' said Marta. 'It was entirely deliberate he chose you rather than anyone here. All his life he kept his story from his sisters. He's not even buried next to them. I think even from the grave he would want to keep this last record secret from his own generation.'

'You know the family has a plot?' said Gerhard. 'In the village where Werner's parents lived. But he insisted he was to be buried here. In Munich.'

'So it's no wonder,' said Marta. 'It's no surprise he chose you.'

Stewart smiled. 'What did he ever see in me? A stupid kid.' A waiter came with a pot of coffee. Stewart waited until he had finished refilling their cups. 'You know,' he said as the waiter moved out of earshot, 'As a boy, I used to love visiting, even though it was a bit spooky. Perhaps because it was spooky. There he was, on his own, all those hidden rooms, all the wartime mementos. And then, when I was older, I felt the exact opposite. He was a symbol of everything wrong with the old world. There he was, so I thought, running his sweatshop like a petty autocrat with his Dickensian workhouse. But I guess ... I guess he surprised us all.'

Stewart looked at them both for a moment, weighing up his next sentence.

'I've been thinking .. ' He rubbed his chin. The others waited. 'I've been wondering whether this might be published. I've typed it all up.'

Marta looked at Gerhard, then back at Stewart. 'Well, I'm sure one of the magazines might pick it up. But ... as I said, you might upset some people.' There was a pause. 'I tell you what. Wait. Wait six months. See how you feel then. If you still want to go ahead with it, contact me and I will see what I can do. Perhaps I might put you in touch with our London office. Yes. They can do it.'

Stewart nodded. They sipped their coffee.

'Tomorrow I'm taking Jane and Alison to see the grave,' he said. 'If we can find it.'

'Has Jane read the diaries?' Marta asked.

'Not the wartime ones. She had a look at the postwar stuff. She was fascinated. The earlier records, I ... I don't know why ... I was just a bit hesitant to show her.'

'I understand,' said Gerhard. 'Give it time.'

'I am really glad she came,' said Marta. 'She's lovely. And Alison's adorable.' She picked up a cake, broke off a piece off and popped it into her mouth.

'Yes,' she repeated. 'I am glad you all came.'

II

The taxi pulled up at the cemetery. Stewart and Jane looked about them. They were on the edge of town where it met the countryside. There was little traffic, a few houses in the distance. A church stood by the cemetery, but they could see even from the car that it was locked, its front door padlocked. The rain had stopped, but the clouds threatened still, and a wind caught the leaves and the scraps of drifting litter.

Stewart guessed they would never find another taxi to take them back, so he haggled with the driver to wait. A price was agreed, and Stewart went to look for the cemetery entrance. They wandered in, then strode up and down the rows of graves. Alison ran off to explore on her own. She soon gave a shout and called them over. Sure enough, she had it, she had found the grave.

Stewart and Jane walked over, and Jane asked Alison to lay some flowers by the headstone. There was no inscription, just a name and the dates of birth and death. They each stood in their own thoughts for a few moments. Presently, Jane took Alison's hand, and the two of them began to walk along the aisle. But Stewart ran after them, and crouched down and said softly to Alison, 'See if you can find two names. One is Hans. The other Christoph. Just see what you can find.' His wife looked down at his daughter and they both turned. Their voices faded as they drifted away.

Stewart walked back to Werner's grave and stood, absolutely still, and he thought once more of his uncle's story. And he thought of the land he now stood on. What would it have been like all those years ago, when great armies clashed in what was the final spasm of the European nightmare? How had this place looked, this cemetery, the street outside, these houses, this neighbourhood. Had it all been smashed, bombed, the buildings levelled, burned to the ground, the fields scarred and ravaged?

And then he thought of the countries of the East, of Poland, of Ukraine, of the great expanses where the catastrophe of war had raged, and he imagined a landscape from some far planet, some reality beyond imagining, etched in black and crimson with the stain of spilt blood, a countryside whose life and whose capacity for giving and supporting life had been expunged by the inferno around it. How had any of this ever been covered up beneath their feet, he thought, how was it that within a generation the carnage had been trodden underfoot by new life, a new civilisation, a new society which built on destroyed land and consigned the past to burial in ignominy, to become an archaeological footnote, to be dug up in some future as one might the remains of the campaigns of an Alexander or a Caesar.

And he thought of the men and women caught up in that struggle, crushed under a wheel of war whose impersonal and implacable momentum could not be broken. He thought of the peasants thrashing about in the no-man's-land between the two empires as their insane leaders struggled for supremacy in this Europe in which he stood, and he recalled the farmers whose blighted crops Werner and his comrades stole in their dash for freedom. He thought of the boy, the soldier, the last Russian to stand in their way before they crossed into the West, and he wondered to himself which outback in the steppes he might have come from. Had his family already suffered in Stalin's great terror? How bitter must have been the parting as this new war wrenched him away to fight and die on the blackened soil of a distant hell. Would they ever, could they ever, have seen his body again, or did it lie where he fell, inert, unburied, forgotten even by his own army, preserved in the ice until the thaw, when nature might have begun to return it to the earth. Watery eyes, a gap-toothed smile, a stupid grin. He thought of the fragility of life, its precious essence, and how ill-equipped nature had left us to defend it against the murderous instincts of our inherited biology. But then a sense of amazement began to grow inside him that in spite of all this a line between Werner and himself had endured, that some amongst them had survived, had progressed, had rebuilt, and miraculously had re-created a world in which he, Stewart, could live and love and create. The intuition grew in him that all history had somehow and despite everything resulted in this, that he could stand here, and see, and think, and breathe. He reached forward and touched the grey stone headpiece of the gravestone with the tips of his fingers. He felt the rough texture of the clay, and as he moved his fingers across it he sensed the exquisitely fine grooves and pockmarks of its surface, the result of years of wind and rain and sun beating against it every second of every day. A dull thunder rippled through the clouds above. He felt the condensation in the sky and the atmosphere about him as it scattered a fine coating of moisture against his face, his neck, his lungs, and against the surface of every plant and stone in the cemetery and the fields around him. He breathed in and perceived with a new clarity the smell of the air and the tang of the leaves and the grass. He looked up as Jane and Alison came walking into view and smiled at them.

'Ali has something to say to you,' his wife said.

'Darling, tell me in the car.'

And, linking arms, the three of them turned and walked back to the waiting taxi.